THE
FRENCH
DETECTION

Other books by Ann Waldron

THE
FRENCH
DETECTION

by Ann Waldron

E. P. DUTTON   NEW YORK

J
W

Library of Congress Cataloging in Publication Data

Waldron, Ann.   The French detection.

SUMMARY: Bored with camp and the other summer
alternatives offered to her, 13-year-old Bessie determines
to go to France on her own. Once there she finds it
full of surprises.
[1. France—Fiction] I. Title.
PZ7.W1465Fr [Fic] 79-10233 ISBN: 0-525-30190-9

Published in the United States by E. P. Dutton, a Division
of Elsevier-Dutton Publishing Company, Inc., New York
Published simultaneously in Canada by Clarke,
Irwin & Company Limited, Toronto and Vancouver
Editor: Ann Durell   Designer: Meri Shardin

Printed in the U.S.A.   First Edition
10 9 8 7 6 5 4 3 2 1

For M. O. W.

BESSIE Hightower had a very strong will. Everybody said so. (Or they said something like "Bessie Hightower sure is pigheaded.") She had red hair and freckles, and she knew what she wanted.

When she wanted to read every book by Louisa May Alcott, she did—even though the library in Delight, Texas, had to get some of them from the interlibrary loan.

"She's very mature for her age," said her mother.

When she was learning to ride horseback and fell off in a dry creek bed, she got right up and climbed back on the horse.

"She's really a tough nut to crack," said her father.

She dived off the high diving board at the swimming pool at the Shamrock hotel in Houston before any of her cousins would do it.

"She's a stem-winder, all right," said her grand-father.

And when her mother insisted she go to the fancy girls' summer camp in the Texas hill country, the one Lynda Bird Johnson had gone to, she stayed for a

1

week and then she left. She walked into Kerrville and caught a bus to Houston, and then she caught the bus to Delight. "It's a waste of time," she told her family. "All that group singing."

"She's inner-directed," said her grandmother, who read a lot of books on psychology.

So when Bessie Hightower said she wanted to go to France, everybody knew she meant it.

But why did she want to go to France?

"I just do," Bessie said. "I really want to go."

And she didn't know exactly why she did want to go. She just wanted to see France.

She had a model of the Eiffel Tower that someone had given her when she was a small child, and she liked that.

She admired a country that produced a woman like Joan of Arc, who wore armor and rode horseback and led an army and heard voices.

And she liked the language. She was taking French that year, in the seventh grade. She liked a language that *surprised* you, the way French did. Words didn't sound the way you thought they would—*fils* was feese. *Mot* was moe. *Suis* was swee. It was interesting.

"But a thirteen-year-old girl can't go to France by herself," Mrs. Hightower said.

"Why don't you go with her, hon?" said Mr. Hightower.

"I can't go running off to France," Mrs. Hightower said crossly. "I have two other children, in case you've forgotten. I can't go running off all over the face of the earth."

"I'll be all right," Bessie said.

"What about camp?" her mother said. "A nice camp.

I saw one advertised in *The New York Times* where you could learn French. A French camp—in New Hampshire or Vermont, one of those."

The Hightowers lived in Delight, Texas, but they read the Sunday *New York Times*. Mr. Hightower brought it home from the office every Thursday—he was the editor of the *Delight Daily Enterprise*.

"I don't want to go to a dumb camp," Bessie said. "I tried camp. Can I go to this place in Dijon, France, and take the summer course there?"

She handed her mother a brochure she'd gotten from the French teacher at school. Her mother looked at it and said, "But, sugar, you have to be sixteen years old to take that course!"

Bessie never gave up.

"What about this place in France?" she asked her mother a few days later. "I found it in the travel section of *The New York Times*."

Mrs. Hightower looked at the tiny advertisement. "Spend 1 month in a small French village for $300," it said, and gave an address in New York to write to.

"Send off for the brochure," said Mrs. Hightower.

"I already did," Bessie said, and she handed it over.

Mrs. Hightower read it carefully. A woman named Lydia Packard and a Frenchman named Philippe Menard were inviting Americans to come to their farmhouse in the village of La Valette in the Berry section of France to learn French and to work at various crafts like pottery and weaving and to go on excursions to points of interest. Each guest had to stay at least one month and had to agree to speak French.

"Do you know that much French?" Mrs. Hightower asked.

3

"She's young—she can pick it up quickly," Mr. Hightower said.

"Well, it does look interesting," Mrs. Hightower said.

"Damned if it doesn't," said Mr. Hightower. "Call up this woman and talk to her. The brochure says she'll be in New York until May first."

Mrs. Hightower talked to Lydia Packard a long time. "She sounds very nice," she reported to Mr. Hightower. "She's an American and she's over here visiting her parents. She sounds like a lovely person."

"What did she say about a thirteen-year-old girl coming?"

"She said they were hoping to have all ages—but that she couldn't be a baby-sitter. I told her Bessie was very mature for her age. And she said in that case, if she wanted to come, she'd be welcome," Mrs. Hightower said. And then she added, "Oh, I don't know!"

"What about drugs?" Mr. Hightower said.

"I didn't ask her about drugs," said Mrs. Hightower.

"Call her back," Mr. Hightower said, "and ask her."

"I can't call up somebody and ask them if they use drugs," Mrs. Hightower said.

"I can," said Mr. Hightower. And he called Lydia Packard and said he wanted to make sure this farmhouse wasn't full of a bunch of drug addicts or Jesus freaks.

He asked a lot of questions, and apparently he didn't make Lydia Packard mad, Bessie was glad to hear. "Well, we'll have to talk it over and we'll let you know," Mr. Hightower said.

And the Hightowers talked it over. And talked it over. And talked it over.

"But she's so young," Mrs. Hightower said.

4

"But she's tough," Mr. Hightower said.

"She *is* mature for her age," Mrs. Hightower said.

"It costs an awful lot," Mr. Hightower said. "Plane fare . . ."

"Not as much as that dumb French camp in Maine or wherever," Bessie said.

"She's right," Mrs. Hightower said.

"She knows what she wants, all right," Mr. Hightower said. "I read somewhere that Henry Luce traveled by himself from China across Europe to the United States when he was only fourteen years old."

"He must have been *very* mature for his age," Mrs. Hightower said.

In the end, they told Bessie she could go to La Valette—if they could figure out a way to get her to New York to catch the plane to Paris.

And then it turned out that Lucy Robbins, Mrs. Hightower's best friend, was going to New York the first of July and would be glad to take Bessie with her and put her on the plane for Paris.

Lucy Robbins was very interested in La Valette. "You know, I think I know Lydia Packard," she said. "I think she was at boarding school with me—remember when Mama made me go east to boarding school? I'm sure it's the same one."

That made everybody—but Bessie—feel better.

Mrs. Hightower was reading the brochure for the thousandth time when she noticed the directions for getting to La Valette.

In Paris, go to the train station called la gare d'Austerlitz. At the ticket booth, ask for the train to Argenton-sur-Creuse. It is on the line going to Limoges and Toulouse. Get off at Argenton and call 47–85–16 from the café. You will be calling the only phone at La Valette. Ask for Lydia Packard. It takes me five minutes to get to the phone. I will come to Argenton to pick you up.

"Why, Bessie can't do that," said Mrs. Hightower.

"She could take a taxi from the airport to the train station in Paris," said Mr. Hightower, but he didn't sound sure of himself.

"And then buy a ticket by herself and get to a strange town and use the telephone in *French!*" Mrs. Hightower was aghast. "I should think *not.* I tell you, she can't do it."

"I can do it," Bessie said. But she wasn't sure she *could* do it. Not at all. Still, she said it again. "I can do it."

"No." Mrs. Hightower was firm.

"There must be a way," Bessie said.

"Maybe we'll think of something," Mr. Hightower said.

Two days later, Mr. Hightower thought of something.

"I can call up Scott Fry and ask him to meet Bessie at the airport and put her on the train for Argenton," he said. "He can call up that lady in La Valette and tell her what train Bessie's on and what time she'll get to Argenton."

"Who's Scott Fry?" Bessie asked.

"He's an old friend of mine from journalism school," Mr. Hightower said. "He works in the Paris bureau of *The New York Times.*"

Bessie prayed he wouldn't be on vacation in July.

6

"I'll have to call him early tomorrow morning—it's seven hours later in Paris than it is in Texas," Mr. Hightower said.

Finally, it was all arranged. Almost all.

Mrs. Hightower wanted to buy Bessie a new dress to wear on the plane.

"I'll wear jeans," Bessie said.

"You can't wear jeans to Paris," Mrs. Hightower said.

"Yes I can," Bessie said, and everybody got ready to give in.

"She knows what she wants," Mr. Hightower said.

But Lucy Robbins put her foot down. "No, ma'am," she said. "You can't go to New York City with me in blue jeans. Everybody up there thinks people from Texas are hicks anyway. If you can't wear a decent dress, I'm not going to take you to Kennedy Airport, and that's final."

Bessie knew when she had met her match. She went to Houston with her mother to buy a two-piece dress at Neiman's, and she found it delightful when the salesladies made a fuss over her when they found out she was going to Paris, France, all by herself, on July 1.

Bessie went over to her grandparents' house to tell them good-bye, and her grandmother looked at her admiringly.

"You've got spunk, Bessie," she said. "I'm proud of you."

"You know, I was in France during the First World War," her grandfather said.

"Did you learn any French?" Bessie asked.

"I learned to say 'Voulez-vous coucher avec moi?' but that wouldn't be any use to you," he said.

7

"You ought to be ashamed of yourself," said Bessie's grandmother.

"What does it mean?" Bessie asked.

"You say it to girls," Bessie's grandfather said. "It means 'Do you want to go to bed with me?' " He chuckled.

Bessie's grandmother gave her a a diary and told her to write in it while she was gone. Her grandfather gave her twenty dollars.

Her mother gave her a French dictionary, and her father bought her an Instamatic.

8

AND it all went smooth as glass.

Mrs. Robbins put her on the plane at Kennedy Airport in New York, and Scott Fry met her in Paris.

Bessie loved the way Mr. Fry looked—sort of tired and bored and sophisticated.

"We have three hours before your train leaves," he said. "What would you like to do? Eat lunch? Go to the Louvre? Ride down the Champs-Elysées?"

"I want to see the Eiffel Tower and I want to ride on the subway," Bessie said.

Mr. Fry said that could be arranged easily enough. "We'll just take a taxi over to the gare d'Austerlitz, buy your train ticket, check your bag, and take the métro— that's the subway—over to the Eiffel Tower," he said. "Off we go."

In the taxi, Mr. Fry spoke to her in French, but Bessie couldn't understand what he said. He seemed surprised that she didn't know any more French than she did.

"How old are you?" he said.

"Thirteen," Bessie said. "But I'm a fast learner— everybody says so."

"You must be," he said. "You're mighty brave to come over here all by yourself."

"I know," Bessie said. She was busy looking out the window. "Paris is funny-looking—not like Houston, or even New York."

"Nobody ever said Paris is funny-looking," said Mr. Fry.

"Oh, I meant it's different-looking," Bessie said. "I like it. The roofs are funny, though."

The roofs were funny and the streets were narrow and all the houses were right on the street, and people were sitting at tables right on the sidewalk, eating. It was great, Bessie thought.

They got to the train station, and Mr. Fry bought Bessie's ticket for her and checked her bag. Then he went to a phone booth and called Lydia Packard—he looked at Bessie over the phone while he waited for Miss Packard to come to the phone—and told her what train Bessie would be on.

"That's all squared away," he said. "Now, off to the Eiffel Tower. Let's go down here and get on the métro."

They came up out of the métro and walked. Bessie could see the Eiffel Tower now and then over the roofs as they walked, and when they got to it, she took out her Instamatic and took a picture of it. She walked all the way around it and announced, "I like it."

"Good," said Mr. Fry. "I certainly am relieved."

They rode the elevator to the top and looked at all Paris spread out before them. Mr. Fry pointed out Notre-Dame and Sacré-Cœur and the Champs-Elysées, and Bessie took more pictures.

They stopped for lunch, and Bessie gazed at the

10

menu dumbfounded. She didn't recognize a single word on it. She pointed and pronounced the words as best she could—and ended up with spinach pancakes which were very good indeed.

They walked to the métro to go back to the train station. Downstairs there was a big crowd on the platform, and the métro train was late in coming. When it finally came, so many people were trying to get on that Mr. Fry was pushed ahead of Bessie. For a moment, she had a horrible feeling that he was going to be swept away from her and the train would leave her on the platform. But somebody behind her gave a tremendous whack on her back that pushed her into the car behind Mr. Fry.

As the doors closed and the train started, she turned around to thank whoever it was who had pushed her onto the train, but no one responded to her smile. It must have been the dark young man right behind her, she decided, but he was edging away from her.

In fact, the train was stopping, and he was getting off at this, the first stop since they'd gotten on.

Bessie was sleepy and suffering from jet lag, and so her mind worked slowly.

They were walking up the stairs at the gare d'Austerlitz when something occurred to her.

She looked in her purse.

"I've been robbed," she announced. "That man stole my billfold."

"What man?" asked Mr. Fry.

"That man that helped me get on the subway," Bessie said. "I thought he was being so nice—and he stole my billfold! What a creep! My new billfold!"

"This is dreadful," said Mr. Fry "I'm afraid it's all too

11

common in the métro. But what a beginning for your trip!"

"Let's go after him," Bessie said. "I know where he got off."

"We'd never find him," Mr. Fry said. "But let's see what we have to do. Did he get your passport?"

"Oh, no, my passport was in the zipper compartment in my purse," Bessie said.

"Traveler's checks?" asked Mr. Fry.

"No, they were in the zipper compartment with my passport," Bessie said.

"Then he just got your money?"

"Oh, money," said Bessie, a little embarrassed. "That's all right. . . ."

"I forgot you're one of those rich Texans," Mr. Fry said.

"It's not that," Bessie said. "It's just that I didn't have any money in my billfold. I put it in my underwear. My granddaddy warned me before I left Delight. But my Advanced Swimmer's card was in my billfold. I hate to lose that. Do you think I'll have to pass the Advanced Swimmer's test again? I want to take Junior Lifesaving when I get back."

"Surely the Red Cross will work something out," said Mr. Fry. "Well, I'm very glad you didn't lose any money. But after this, Bessie, keep your purse closed and under your arm when you're in a crowd."

At the railroad station, Bessie went into the ladies' room and got her money from where it was pinned to her underwear and put some in her purse. Just in case, she left some where it was.

Meanwhile, Mr. Fry had gotten her bag, and he led her down the platform to her train.

"Now, listen for the station," he said. "Argenton comes right after Châteauroux. When the conductor calls Châteauroux, begin to get ready. Get your bag and go stand at the end of the corridor. French trains don't stop long in the station."

Bessie promised to listen.

Mr. Fry put her in a compartment, pointing out that European trains were different from American trains. Bessie did not tell him she had never been on any train at all.

At last Mr. Fry left.

Bessie was delighted to be on her own at last.

B<small>ESSIE</small>, on her own, found she was very sleepy.

It was 1:30 P.M. in Paris, and although it was only 6:30 A.M. in Texas, she'd still been up all night. As she waited for the train to start, her head began to fall over and her eyes began to close. She jerked awake, though, when five young people in blue jeans and tee-shirts came into the compartment and began stuffing backpacks and sleeping bags in the baggage racks. They had a tape deck on which an old Beatles song was playing loudly. They took out a bottle of wine and passed it around with a box of cookies. They offered both to Bessie, but she was afraid to drink any wine. She took some cookies, however, and after quite a lot of effort at conversation, she discovered they were German.

They couldn't talk much—the Germans didn't know much English and she knew no German and neither could understand the other's French—but the Germans all smiled a lot and kept passing Bessie cookies. Bessie fought off sleep and smiled at the Germans and looked out the window. France seemed to be full of nothing but green fields, houses with red-tiled roofs, and white cows. She munched cookies.

When the train came to Châteauroux, the Germans got her bag down from the rack and carried it for her to the end of the car.

"Bah!" they shouted at Bessie as she got down at Argenton. "Bah!" They waved.

It took Bessie a minute to figure out that they were saying "Bye," and then she waved back.

Inside the station, she looked for Miss Packard, but the only person who wasn't meeting somebody was a skinny girl in blue jeans and a halter top. Bessie thought she looked American, and wondered what she was doing in Argenton. Then the girl came over and said, "Bessie Hightower? Ça va? Je suis Lydia Packard."

Was this Miss Packard? Miss Packard who had been to boarding school with Mrs. Robbins? Mrs. Robbins was forty years old and Lydia Packard looked like a high-school girl. And not a high-school girl that Bessie's mother would approve of, either.

She was certainly not the kind of grown-up, schoolteachery person that Bessie had been expecting. She looked, in fact, like a hippie.

Bessie was trying to digest all this while Miss Packard was talking in French. And Bessie could not understand her French any more than she had been able to understand the Germans' German.

She followed Miss Packard across the parking lot, and Lydia—Bessie quit thinking of her as Miss Packard—stopped beside a little old beat-up station wagon and threw Bessie's suitcase through the rear window.

Bessie, still silent—silent for perhaps the longest time in her life—sat in the front seat beside Lydia as they drove away from the train station and down the narrow streets of Argenton. Lydia chatted pleasantly in

15

French, but Bessie was too dazed to try to find out what she was talking about.

They drove out of Argenton, past pale-looking little houses that opened right on the road, and then they were in the country. Everything looked much tidier and smaller than the Texas countryside. There were hedges along the road instead of barbed-wire fences, and the houses seemed to be clustered together in little villages instead of spread out like proper ranch houses.

After hurtling along for a while, they turned down a very narrow dirt road that ran between even taller hedges, and then they suddenly pulled to a stop in front of a bunch of long low stucco houses with red-tiled roofs. They were parked beside a big manure heap.

Lydia got out and got Bessie's suitcase.

"On est là," Lydia said, and Bessie followed her through a low doorway into a long, dark room full of strange people.

There was a lot of chatter in incomprehensible French, and Bessie had no idea who anybody was. They smiled at her. There were two young men with long hair and beards. (More hippies, thought Bessie with a little excitement.) There were some girls, older girls, apparently both French and American, she thought.

The room was so dim she couldn't tell much about it at first. The floor was bumpy—it was made of stone—and everybody was sitting around a long table in the back of the room. There was a huge fireplace on one side and a little kitchen up at the front of the room by the door.

There was a ladder going up to a loft, and Lydia

took Bessie up there and showed her her quarters—a
little mattress lying on the floor in one corner. The
roof sloped steeply, and Bessie could see the sky
through cracks between the tiles.

"What happens when it rains?" she asked Lydia.

"Oh, it doesn't leak," Lydia said. "The tiles overlap. I
know it looks like there are holes in the roof, but it's
quite tight, actually."

There were some looms in the loft, and another mattress. Somebody named Marie-Claude slept there,
Lydia said. Bessie put her suitcase down beside her
mattress and climbed back down the ladder after
Lydia.

Lydia showed her the rest of the house. There was a
tiny darkroom opening off the big dining room–
kitchen, and another bedroom. There were some more
rooms under the same roof, but you had to go outdoors to get to them.

There was a shower outside—which Lydia called la
douche, and Bessie thought that was hilarious—and
a privy.

"It's very simple," Lydia explained, "but it's better
than it was. There wasn't even hot water or a privy
when we rented the place."

Bessie was surprised, but intrigued. It was more like
camping than that girls' camp had been, she thought.

"At least you don't have to wash a bathtub or clean a
toilet," she said.

Lydia looked pleased and showed her the shed
room, where there were lots of bicycles and a potter's
wheel.

She was showing Bessie the vegetable garden when
the police arrived. They came in a sunny yellow van,

and there were two of them. They wore khaki uniforms and funny hats that were round with flat tops. The caps looked like dogs' water dishes, Bessie decided, that had little brims.

The policemen got out of the van, and Lydia went over to meet them. They talked in French which Bessie could not understand.

The police followed Lydia into the main room, and Bessie trailed after them. There was more talk in French, and then a general movement out of the room.

"They want to see everybody's papers," Lydia explained. "Get your passport, Bessie."

Bessie clambered up the ladder and got her passport and brought it back down. One of the policemen took it and went out to the van and began talking on his radio. Lydia explained he was calling in the passport numbers to Paris, to see if any of the Americans were wanted for anything.

Well, this is exciting, thought Bessie. Kind of like a spy movie on television. The police had never come to their home in Delight. France definitely had more going on than Texas.

The other policeman was checking the identity cards of the French people. That didn't take near as long as checking all the American passport numbers did.

It turned out everybody's papers were okay, and then the policemen talked to Lydia and to one of the young Frenchmen a lot. He was the Philippe Menard mentioned in the ad, Bessie found out.

Lydia did most of the talking. She even took the policemen around the house and showed them the douche and the vegetable garden.

Bessie followed, just in case she could understand what they were talking about. But she couldn't. It sounded like they were always saying "Honk-honk-honk-honk."

At last the policemen got in their little yellow van and drove away. Lydia came in and sat down at the table with everybody else.

"What was all that about?" asked Bessie, interrupting a lively discussion in French.

"Oh, they just love to come and check out all the Americans," Lydia said. She spoke casually, but she looked strained. "They never have seen many Americans around here before."

They all started talking French again, and everyone got very excited. Bessie gave up trying to understand what they were saying. What good had it done to study French so hard at Delight Junior High School if she couldn't understand what they said in France?

"I'm going to take a nap," she said, and went up the ladder to her loft.

She sat down on her mattress and opened her suitcase. There was definitely a mystery here. And how could she find out what was going on when she couldn't understand French? Well, she'd just have to learn French in a hurry. First, she'd better write home and tell her folks she'd gotten here all right.

Dear Mama and Papa, she wrote, *La Valette is very interesting. Miss Packard is very nice. The others are neat, too.* Was that actually a lie? Bessie wondered. They certainly weren't neat if, by *neat,* you meant clean and tidy. Oh, well. *I am going to learn a lot while I'm here. . . .*

She fell asleep before she finished it.

W HEN Bessie woke up from her nap, she was very hungry.

She lay on her mattress looking up at the roof of the loft and the spots of blue sky scattered among the tiles, and listened to voices coming up from downstairs.

They were talking French. She couldn't understand one word they were saying, but she liked the way it sounded. She stretched and decided she had to get something to eat.

She stood up, shook out the skirt to her dress, decided to change into blue jeans, and looked around for a place to hang up her dress.

There wasn't any place.

Good, thought Bessie. No closets to fool with. She stuffed the dress in the suitcase and pulled out jeans and a tee-shirt.

Then she went down the ladder.

"Salut, Bess-ee!"

Everybody greeted her. They were all sitting around the big table. "As-tu bien dormi? Bonjour!"

"Bonjour," Bessie said, and headed outside for the

latrine. In a minute she was back, and she slid onto a bench at the table.

"What time is it?" she asked.

"Onze heures," said Lydia.

Bessie looked blank

"Eleven o'clock," Lydia said.

"It's still light at eleven?" Bessie asked.

Lydia translated what she said into French, and everybody laughed.

"It's morning," Lydia explained. "You've been asleep since yesterday afternoon."

"I never slept so long in my life," Bessie said. "I can't believe it. I guess it's jet lag."

"Enough English," Lydia said. "Assez d'anglais. Du café, Bessie?" She stood up, holding a pot in one hand and a heavy pitcher in the other, and poured from both of them at the same time into a big cup and handed that to Bessie.

"Du café?" she repeated.

"No thanks," Bessie said. "I don't drink coffee."

"En français," Lydia said.

"Merci," Bessie said. "Non." She hesitated. "Je ne drink pas le café."

"Je ne bois pas le café," Lydia corrected her.

The girl sitting next to Bessie—her name was Lisa— pushed a loaf of French bread down the table toward her. Bessie looked at it blankly for a minute. It wasn't even on a plate—just a naked loaf of bread on the table.

"I don't eat much breakfast," Bessie said, thinking she would be as little trouble as possible. "Just some cereal and orange juice."

"En français," said Lydia.

21

"I can't," said Bessie. "I mean—well, I'll just have some cereal and orange juice."

"En français," said Lydia.

"Je ne sais pas," said Bessie, ecstatic to remember the phrase for "I don't know."

"We don't have cereal," Lydia said. "French people eat bread and butter and jam and coffee with milk for breakfast."

"An egg?" said Bessie.

"French people never eat eggs for breakfast," said Lydia firmly.

"Okay," Bessie said.

"En français," said Lydia.

"Je ne sais pas," said Bessie.

"D'accord," said Lydia.

"That means okay?" Bessie asked.

"Oui," Lydia said.

"D'accord," said Bessie. Well, that was settled. She reached over and picked up the loaf of bread and tore off a big piece, put butter on it, added strawberry jam, and took a bite. It was delicious.

Everyone was smiling at her and nodding. They were trying to show they were friendly, she decided, in spite of the language barrier.

Bessie smiled and nodded back and ate more of the crusty bread.

"Voudrais-tu du lait, Bessie?" Lydia asked.

Now what? thought Bessie. She pulled another useful phrase out of her memory. "Je ne comprends pas." I don't understand.

"Voudrais-tu," repeated Lydia slowly, "would you like . . . du lait? Some milk?"

"Oui," said Bessie.

Everyone smiled at Bessie. Philippe turned to Lydia and spoke in French. "Honk-honk."

"D'accord," said Lydia. "Philippe says I ought to let you get your first meal without insisting on French. Would you like some milk? I should have known you were too young for coffee."

Bessie did not want them to think she was too young for *anything*, but she also hated the taste of coffee, so she said she'd have some milk.

"Du lait," said Lydia, handing her a cup of milk.

"Du lait," repeated Bessie. "Merci." She turned up the cup and took a big swallow—and spit it out.

"It's not cold," she said. "Ugh."

"Of course it's not cold," Lydia said. "We get it fresh from the cow of Madame Poulet every morning. Right after it's milked."

"Ugh," Bessie said again. "I'm sorry I spit it out." She began to wipe up the milk from the table with her hand. "But I really don't want any. Thank you. Merci."

"Du thé?" Lydia asked.

"Je ne comprends pas," Bessie said.

"Tea?" Lydia said. "Hot tea?"

"No, thank you," said Bessie. "I'll just eat bread." She tore off another big piece and spread it with butter and jam.

Philippe was talking earnestly to Lydia in French, and Lydia laughed and said something to him. Then she spoke to Bessie in English.

"Philippe says maybe you'd like to have hot chocolate. That's what French children have for breakfast."

Bessie thought of saying firmly that she was not a child, but hot chocolate sounded so lovely that the thought was very brief.

"I adore hot chocolate," she said.

"J'adore le chocolat," said Lydia, and she went over to the stove.

"I'm glad you thought of chocolate," Bessie said to Philippe. "Thanks a lot."

"Il ne comprend pas," Lisa said. "Philippe doesn't understand English."

"Merci," Bessie said to him, wishing she could say a little more than that. She ate bread and butter and jam. Breakfast here was like a picnic, she thought. No plates. Just tearing bread off the loaf and eating it.

When Lydia brought the hot chocolate, it was thick and sweet, and Bessie loved it.

"French cuisine is pretty good," she said, and Lydia translated for the others, who laughed and talked to Bessie in French which she couldn't understand.

When she was no longer so hungry, she took time to look around the table at the people and sort them out.

There was Lydia, with her long hair twisted into a knot on top of her head. She was thin and full of energy, and seemed nice enough, even though she was strict, Bessie decided. How could anybody so young be so strict?

And there was Philippe. He was really nice, she thought. He had suggested the hot chocolate. He had curly black hair and a beard and a terrific smile. He ran the place with Lydia. And he looked young, too.

There was Lisa, an American, who was a student at Smith College. She looked like the girls at camp, Bessie decided, only a little older.

Marie-Claude was French and she looked it. She had hennaed hair. She wore a long brocade skirt, boots, and a heavy crocheted sweater. Bessie loved the way she looked. She couldn't help but stare at her whenever she got the chance. She was beautiful.

There were two other French guys. Edouard sat next to Lisa and seemed to like her a lot. He didn't have a beard, and his hair was hennaed like Marie-Claude's. Bessie had never seen a man with hennaed hair before, and she was intrigued. She'd have to learn the French for *henna* so she could ask Lydia about it. Hair was *cheveux,* she knew that much.

The other French kid was François. He didn't say much. François and Edouard were friends of Philippe's and lived in another little village some distance away.

All of them were different from anybody Bessie Hightower had ever known—except Lisa. Lisa was just another American and rather boring.

Bessie gathered from what little French she could understand that Lisa was the last of the Americans who had spent June at La Valette. She was leaving the next day. The other Americans for July would be arriving soon.

"Bessie, il faut choisir un programme de travail," said Lydia.

"What?"

"En français," said Lydia.

Bessie gulped. "Qu'est-ce que c'est?" she asked.

"Il faut," Lydia said, and then, very slowly, one word at a time, explained in French that it was necessary that Bessie choose a work project for the month. It could be weaving or pottery or art.

"Too much like camp," Bessie said.

"En français," Lydia said.

"Oh, never mind," Bessie said.

"En français," Lydia said sternly.

"Pas important," Bessie said, at last.

"Bien," Lydia said. And then she went on in French: Which would it be? Would Bessie like to weave? Throw pots?

Bessie shook her head. "Non."

Then Philippe made another suggestion.

"Photographie?" he said.

"Photography! Yes!" Bessie said.

"En français," Lydia said.

Good grief, thought Bessie. This was going to be very hard—but it was also kind of exciting, like a full-time ongoing game of charades, where you had to have your wits about you every minute.

"Photographie, oui," she said.

"Bien," Lydia said. They told her to bring her appareil, which was apparently the word for *camera,* and she scrambled up to the attic.

When Philippe saw her Instamatic, he smiled and spoke to Lydia in French.

Lydia explained to Bessie that Philippe's darkroom equipment did not include the small reels for the Instamatic's film, but that he would try to buy one. Perhaps, if she did well at learning how to develop and print her own pictures, she would like to borrow a better camera from Philippe.

"Okay," Bessie said.

"En français," Lydia said.

"D'accord," Bessie said. "You know, we never learned how to say useful things like 'd'accord' at Delight Junior High. All we ever learned was things like 'Où est Sylvie?' 'A la piscine,' " she added gloomily.

"You're going to do fine," Lydia said in English. "But we have to be strict, or everybody just relaxes and talks English and never learns any French."

26

"Okay," said Bessie. "I mean, d'accord."

"Bon," said Lydia, and then went on to suggest that Bessie work out a definite photography project with Philippe. She could make a portfolio of photographs of French village life, for instance.

"D'accord," Bessie said.

"But do you have black-and-white film?" Lydia asked. "Most people bring color—and you can't develop that yourself."

"My father got me black-and-white film," Bessie said. "That's what newspapers use."

Everybody was still sitting at the table when a tiny van drove up outside the front door, almost to the doorstep, and stopped in a cloud of dust. The driver blew the horn loudly and then got out.

It was the postman. Lydia went to the door, and he handed her the mail. Lydia walked over to the table, dealt out everybody's letters, and opened one herself.

She exclaimed in horror. She talked rapidly in French to Marie-Claude and Philippe. Édouard and François and Lisa listened and joined in a French chorus of outrage and despair.

"What is it?" Bessie asked. "Qu'est-ce que c'est?"

Everyone answered her at once, and she understood nothing. It all sounded like "Honk-honk-honk-honk." Then the word *impôt* was repeated over and over.

"It's the income tax," Lydia said to her. "We've got to pay this enormous income tax. And we don't have any income at all hardly."

"C'est Malignon," Marie-Claude said, her eyes narrowed.

"Who's Malignon?" Bessie asked. No one answered her. Philippe and Marie-Claude and Lydia were deep in serious conference again.

"Qui est Malignon?" Bessie asked.

"Oh, poor Bessie," Lydia said, breaking off the conference. "Malignon is a man who's trying to get us evicted."

It took Bessie a while to understand it all, or any of it, for that matter, but Lydia explained that Malignon, for some unknown reason, had been trying to make them move out. He was responsible for the frequent visits from the police, and now, Lydia was sure, for this communication about the income tax.

Bessie knew enough to know that income tax was bad news. Apparently in France it was even worse news than in Texas.

"Philippe and I are going to Châteauroux to see a lawyer," Lydia said. She rushed around and disappeared into her bedroom, and reappeared wearing a dress instead of blue jeans. Philippe changed his shirt and combed his hair.

They set off, looking grim.

"Quelle histoire!" said Marie-Claude in a voice of doom.

Bessie liked the phrase, and repeated it several times: "Quelle histoire."

After Lydia and Philippe had gone, Lisa and François and Edouard decided to drive over to Edouard's house.

Marie-Claude, it seemed, was going to Delle, the nearest small town.

"Je vais à vélo," Marie-Claude said to Bessie. "Veux-tu venir?"

"Huh?" said Bessie.

Marie-Claude patiently repeated it a word at a time, pantomiming riding a bicycle, until Bessie understood she was going on a bicycle and did Bessie want to come?

"Sure," said Bessie.

"En français," said Lisa. She was a lot like a camp counselor, Bessie decided.

"What's French for *sure?*" Bessie asked.

"*Certainement,*" Lisa said.

"Certainement," Bessie said. She and Marie-Claude got bicycles, and she followed Marie-Claude down the lane to the paved road and then along the road, between hedges and pastures full of hay and wild flowers.

I'm in France, Bessie told herself. I'm really in France. And it is very, very different from Texas. If only I could speak French better and understand what they say better.

She watched Marie-Claude, who was a little ahead of her, and she loved the easy, graceful way Marie-Claude rode the old bicycle. Bessie was having a little trouble with hers. She was used to a ten-speed and this was a one-speed, but at least it had hand brakes.

They met an old woman dressed in black, driving a flock of geese along the road, and they stopped and held their bikes while the old woman and her charges moved slowly past them.

"Bonjour, madame," Marie-Claude said.

"Bonjour, mademoiselle," the old woman said. "Bonjour."

Then they rode along the top of a ridge and could look across the fields of hay and see the other fields of hay and pastures dotted with tiny white cows grazing in the distance. Here and there, they could see little villages, clusters of houses with red-tiled roofs gathered around a little church with a tall steeple. It all looked rather like some pictures Bessie had seen in the Houston Museum of Fine Arts.

It wasn't far to Delle, and they were soon pedaling up the main street. Marie-Claude spoke to everyone they passed.

"Do you know everybody?" Bessie asked her.

Marie-Claude looked puzzled, and Bessie realized she'd have to ask it in French. But she knew how to say it.

"Connais-tu tout le monde?" she said.

Marie-Claude still looked puzzled. Bessie said it again.

30

"Oh, non, non," she laughed. And she rattled off an explanation which Bessie finally figured out meant that everybody spoke to everybody else in the country.

Marie-Claude stopped and propped her bike up outside the door of a shop that had a sign, BOULANGERIE.

Bessie remembered that meant bakery. I'd have known it anyway, she thought, because of the piles of long loaves of French bread in the window.

She watched and listened while Marie-Claude bought loaves of bread and a cake. Then she went with her to another store, a grocery store, where Marie-Claude bought four bottles of wine.

Marie-Claude put the bread and the cake in Bessie's bicycle basket and the wine in the box tied to her own rear fender, and they set out.

They didn't turn around, Bessie noticed, but went straight down the main street and out of town on the other side.

Marie-Claude was pedaling furiously. She turned around and called out something to Bessie and laughed, beckoning her on with a toss of her head.

Bessie followed, and they hit a long hill. It was a glorious coast down the long, steep hill. At the bottom they went through a tiny little village, turned to the left, and threaded their way down a lane that ran through a forest, then between more pastures, and then came back to the road to La Valette.

"That was fun," Bessie told Marie-Claude when they got home. "C'est amusant."

Marie-Claude smiled and bustled into the house with the wine, and Bessie followed with the bread and cake.

Then she followed Marie-Claude out of doors again, where Marie-Claude went in the garden and pulled up lettuces and picked some green beans.

Bessie had never seen such beautiful green beans.

She helped Marie-Claude string the beans, watched her start cooking lunch, and then wandered back outside to look around the house and village.

Behind their house were three or four other houses—all of them long and low, with red-tiled roofs. People were always coming and going. Just then a boy with a fishing pole over his shoulder walked past her toward the road, and he turned back to stare at her.

"Salut," he said.

"Salut," Bessie said.

Two women were standing in front of another house, talking. A tiny girl played around their feet. A dog tied to a post barked. A man drove a tractor out of a barn and went out to the road.

What can I take pictures of? she wondered. Well, everything, she guessed. She got her camera and went out and took a picture of their house. Then she walked back and smiled and nodded at the ladies and said "Bonjour," and they said "Bonjour" to her and rattled off French which she couldn't understand. And she asked—in pantomime—if she could take a picture of the little girl.

"Oui, certainement," the ladies said. "Elle s'appelle Gabrielle."

Bessie knelt on the ground and took a picture of Gabrielle.

The sun felt warm, and the air smelled good. Bessie went over to look at some rabbits in cages against a wall, took their picture, and walked past Lydia's garden to a tiny little apple orchard. It had only three apple trees, but they were loaded with green apples.

"Bess-ee!"

Marie-Claude was calling her, and Bessie went inside. Marie-Claude handed her a knife and said, "Couteau," and waited for Bessie to repeat it.

Then she handed her a bowl of potatoes and said, "Pommes de terre," and waited. Bessie said it, but Marie-Claude made her say it over and over until she had it just right.

Bessie gathered she was to peel the potatoes, and she did, while Marie-Claude gave her a French lesson. She held up everything in the kitchen and pronounced its name, and made Bessie say it after her.

Well, thought Bessie, it beats camp. And I'll know more French than Miss Mabry. Miss Mabry was the French teacher at Delight Junior High.

Lunch was very late, because Philippe and Lydia were gone a long time. Bessie thought it was the best food she'd ever eaten. The others drank wine, but she drank orange soda—it was warm—which Philippe and Lydia had brought from Châteauroux.

Philippe had also bought a reel for the Instamatic film.

Lydia got a phone call. Mme Poulet, who lived in the nearest house, just down the lane, came to call her to the telephone. She had the only phone in the village, and Bessie later learned that the government paid her a little money to take messages for people who didn't have phones.

Lydia came back and reported that another American was at the railroad station in Argenton. Bessie went with her to meet the newcomer, who turned out to be an old lady. Not an old, white-haired lady, but a lady who was older than Bessie's mother. Her name was

Mamie, her children were grown, and she claimed to love everything.

She spoke French, but Bessie didn't think it was very good French. If I can understand it, then it's not any good, she thought. Everything was "très joli," even the railroad station at Argenton, the town of Argenton, the road to La Valette, the flowers, the cows, the pigs, the farms, and La Valette.

Lydia put Mamie with Lisa in a big bedroom at the end of the house. It had its own fireplace and a rough stone floor. "Très joli," Mamie said. "Très charmant."

Lisa and Edouard were back, and supper was delayed because all the people from the village came to tell Lisa good-bye.

The two ladies Bessie had seen came. And Mme Poulet. And two real old guys named Jacques and Joseph. Joseph brought a basket of mushrooms.

The boy Bessie had seen with the fishing pole came. His name was Thierry.

Everybody except Thierry patted Bessie on the head. "They think your hair is beautiful," Lydia explained. "The French are mad for red hair." Thierry just stared. Then he said something in French, but Bessie didn't know what it was.

"He wants to know if you play football," Lydia said.

"Non," Bessie said.

Bessie gathered that some of the village people knew all about Malignon, because she heard his name mentioned. And *gendarmes*, which she knew was police. And then *impôt*. Lydia talked very earnestly with the man who had driven the tractor. The man's wife put her arm around Lydia and seemed to be trying to cheer her up.

Then Thierry said something else to Bessie, and she didn't understand that either. He pulled on Lydia's arm until she translated for him.

"He wants to know if you can explain to him how American football works," Lydia said.

"Sure," said Bessie. But then she hesitated. Of course, she knew about football. Everybody in Texas knew about football. But how could you explain it to a kid who didn't know any English?

"I'll try," she said. "Come outside." She motioned to Thierry, and he followed her outside. She got a stick off the compost pile and began to trace a rectangle in the sandy soil of the yard.

"Here's the field," she said.

"Qu'est-ce que c'est?" Thierry asked, puzzled.

"Oh, shoot," Bessie said. "Wait a minute." She went into the house and got her French dictionary and came back out. She looked up *field* and then she said to Thierry, pointing at the rectangle, "Champ. C'est le champ."

"Oui," said Thierry, nodding.

Then she looked up *goal*, and pointed toward the goal line, and said, "But." (*But* rhymed with *pew*, and that was funny, Bessie thought.) It was slow work, looking up every word, but she kept at it. *Touchdown* was very hard—it wasn't in the dictionary. *Toucher-bas* somehow didn't sound right, but Thierry didn't mind. At last, he said, "Je comprends," and thanked her.

Bessie wasn't sure at all that he did "comprend," but she had done her best.

She asked him how old he was. ("Quel âge as-tu?" was one of the first phrases she'd learned at Delight Junior High.) She was surprised to find out he was only a year younger than she was, because he was so much smaller.

She went back inside. The company left, and they all sat down to an omelette. Bessie wiped up her plate with French bread, the way everybody else did, and then ate the bread. They had cake for dessert and used the same plates. It was a good system, Bessie thought. She would recommend it to her mother when she got home. It sure saved on dishwashing.

If it wasn't for this business about Malignon, she thought, everything would be perfect.

THE next morning, Mamie was still exclaiming how "beau" and how "joli" everything was. Lydia didn't have to urge her to speak French—she spoke French whenever she talked, and she talked all the time.

Lydia didn't have to tell her to start on a programme du travail, either. She wanted to draw, and she set to work right away, drawing a picture of the house.

She was outside drawing when the postman pulled up with a squeal and a whirlwind of dust.

There were lots of letters, and one with an official stamp that Lydia opened and read. She burst into tears.

"Ma carte de séjour!" she said to Philippe. "On dit qu'elle expire. . . ."

Bessie couldn't stand it. "What is it? Qu'est-ce que c'est?"

The authorities said that Lydia must leave France. Her carte de séjour, her permission to stay in France, had expired.

"They've never bothered me about it before," she said. "I know it's that old Malignon."

37

She decided to go to Mme Poulet's to call the lawyer. She wiped her eyes, found her purse, smoothed her hair, and dashed off.

She came back in a few minutes and said there was another American on her way to Argenton. She would pick her up after she dropped Lisa off at the little town where she was going to stay with some friends of her parents.

"Allons, Bessie et Mamie," she said. "Saint-Benoît-du-Sault est une ville du Moyen Age. Vous l'aimerez."

Bessie wasn't sure what that meant, but she went along.

Saint-Benoît-du-Sault was like nothing Bessie had ever seen before. The streets were so narrow they had to park in a square and walk to the house where Lisa was going to stay. There was a big gate at one end of the narrow street, and little towers on either side of it. Rooms jutted out from the second stories of the houses, so the street was shadowy.

"I love it," Bessie said.

"C'est une ville du Moyen Age," Lydia said.

"Qu'est-ce que c'est?"

"It's a medieval town, a town of the Middle Ages," said Lydia.

"You mean knights in armor came riding down this street?"

"I'm sure they did," Lydia said.

"Stupendous," Bessie said. "How old is this town?"

"Du douzième siècle," Lydia said.

"Je ne comprends pas," Bessie said.

"The twelfth century," Lydia said. "Bessie, you make me talk English too much."

But Bessie was thinking. If Saint-Benoît-du-Sault was

built in the 1100s, that meant it was eight hundred years old. It was older than the Alamo.

Mamie was about to wet her pants exclaiming over everything. She wanted to sketch the gate at the end of the street. Lydia said that was fine.

"Bessie et moi, nous allons aller à la *Patisserie et Salon de Thé*," Lydia said.

They went to a shop with windows filled with plates piled high with cakes and cookies.

"Bonjour," Lydia said to the lady behind the counter.

"Bonjour, madame et mademoiselle," the lady said.

Lydia looked at the display of cakes and cookies in the glass case, pointed to a little cake, and said something to the lady. The lady took it out and put it on a plate. So Bessie pointed to a big cake with lots of chocolate, and the lady put a piece of that one on a plate.

They took their plates to a little table and sat down, and the lady came to take their order for drinks. Lydia said she'd have "du thé," and asked Bessie if she, too, wanted tea.

"Do they have iced tea?" Bessie asked.

"I'll ask," Lydia said, and asked in French. The lady said, "Non. Pas de glace." No ice.

"Would you like hot tea?" Lydia asked.

"Does she have a Coke?" Bessie asked.

"Avez-vous du Co-ca-Co-la?" Lydia asked, accenting all the syllables alike, and Bessie made a note of how to say it. She might want to order one herself some time.

"She does have Coke," Lydia said.

"Oh, good," Bessie said.

They began to eat their cake, and Bessie thought hers was perhaps the best thing she had ever eaten in all her life—it seemed to have thirteen layers of chocolate cake with chocolate filling, chocolate whipped cream, and chocolate icing.

The lady brought the drinks, and Bessie sipped her Coke. She didn't spit it out, but she made a face.

"What's the matter?" Lydia asked.

"It's awful," Bessie said. "It's warm."

Lydia shrugged.

"This is the only thing I don't like about France," Bessie said. "You can't get anything with ice, or anything that's cold."

"Sometimes you can," Lydia said. "But in France they don't have refrigerators like the ones in America. Things aren't ever as cold. You'll just have to drink water."

"I believe I'll have another piece of cake, and a glass of water," Bessie said.

"En français," Lydia said.

"D'accord," Bessie said. "How do you ask for water?"

"Un verre d'eau," Lydia said.

"Un verre d'eau," Bessie said.

"S'il vous plaît," Lydia said.

"S'il vous plaît," Bessie said. "That means *please.*"

Bessie went over to the counter and pointed at the cake, and the woman smiled and put another piece of it on another little plate for Bessie. And then Bessie said, "Un verre d'eau, s'il vous plaît."

The woman looked puzzled and rattled off some French. "Honk-honk-honk-honk."

"Un verre d'eau, s'il vous plaît," Bessie said, more carefully this time. She pantomimed drinking a glass of something.

The woman smiled and exclaimed with delight. "Un

40

verre d'eau, mademoiselle. Tout de suite." She brought a glass of water to the table.

Bessie didn't eat. She sat there with her chin on her hand, her elbow on the table.

"What's the matter?" Lydia asked.

"I can't understand what they say and they can't understand what I say," Bessie said. "I feel like a dope. And I never felt like a dope in my whole, entire life."

"Oh, for heaven's sake!" Lydia said. "It will come. Lisa didn't understand anything either when she got here. When I first got to France I couldn't understand what they said, and I thought I knew French. And I'd had six years of French in junior and senior high school. Don't feel bad. You just have to keep trying. Just quit talking English. You're a tough kid. You'll do all right."

Bessie began to eat. "You had trouble, too?" she said. "And you're so good at it now. I can't believe it."

"You better believe it," Lydia said.

"How did you get to come to France?" Bessie asked her.

"I got hooked on France when I was a kid," Lydia said. "We took a vacation in Martinique, and I was fascinated with the language. I loved it in high school, and I always had good teachers. When I finished high school, my parents let me come to France with a friend that summer, and we stayed and got jobs in the grape harvest. That was awful. We had to work twelve hours a day for about two dollars, and we slept in crowded dormitories and there wasn't any hot water. But I knew I wanted to stay in France. I got a job working on the restoration of a castle. You paid *them* two dollars a day, and in return you got your room and board and got to

41

work on the castle. I worked up on scaffolding, and right away I learned better French. I had to be able to say *higher* and *lower*. My life depended on it.

"That's where I met Philippe—at the castle," she added, smiling.

"And you never went back to America?"

"Oh, I went back," Lydia said. "My parents made me come home after I'd been here a year. I even went to college in America for a year. I hated it. I wanted to be back in France. So I came back and went to the castle. Philippe and I had the idea to do this—run a pension-étagère, a boardinghouse and craft workshop combined, for Americans who wanted to learn French and meet French people."

"What made you settle in La Valette?" Bessie asked.

"Well, we had bicycles, and we decided to take a bicycle camping trip in the Berry—it was a section Philippe had always wanted to know more about. He had a friend—that's Edouard—who lived near here, and we went to see him. Edouard knew that the man who was renting our house at La Valette was going to move, and he told us about it. We came over and rented it right away. We loved the countryside and La Valette.

"We moved in, and we spent all winter fixing it up. We put all the money both of us could scrape up into it. Philippe made the shower and the darkroom and the potter's wheel. We put in hot water. The people in the village were wonderful to us. They love to have Americans come.

"Then I went home this spring and put ads in *The New York Times* and stayed with my parents to answer the letters and phone calls that came in. Then I came back—and we persuaded Marie-Claude to help us."

42

Bessie was awed. She had never met anybody so young—Lydia was only twenty—who had done so much. Once more, she propped her chin on her hand, but this time she gazed at Lydia admiringly.

"And it works," Bessie said. "You run the whole thing."

"It worked—up until the time Malignon started hounding us." Lydia poured the last of her tea into the cup and stirred more sugar into it. She looked very sad, and suddenly rather frail to Bessie.

"Who is Malignon exactly?" Bessie asked.

"He's an important businessman in the neighborhood," Lydia said. "He has an antique store and a gift shop. And a big pottery, too. You know, some of the clay around here is wonderful. He sells his pottery at the gift shop, and he exports a lot. He has a finger in lots of pies."

"Where does he hang out?" Bessie asked. "I mean, where does he have his shop?"

"In Couronne," Lydia said. "That's a town on the other side of La Valette. It's bigger than Delle, but not as big as Argenton or Châteauroux."

"But I don't understand why he wants to get you out of the house," Bessie said.

"We don't understand it either," Lydia said. "He complains to the police that too many people live there . . . that too many Americans come there . . . that we all take drugs . . . that we all have group sex. There are never too many people there. None of us ever use drugs—Philippe won't allow them on the place. And as for group sex—well, that's ridiculous."

"But can't you prove he's wrong?" Bessie asked.

"We prove he's wrong about one thing," Lydia said,

43

"and then he comes up with something else. And it's maddening—the harassment."

"What made him notice you in the first place?" Bessie asked. "I mean, how did this start?"

"Somebody said he wants our house for his secretary to live in," Lydia said. "I don't know. But the old woman who owns our house used to be his nurse, and he has a lot of influence with her. She was glad to rent it to us last summer, and now she's trying to get us out." Lydia stirred her tea.

"We have an oral lease, and that's supposed to be binding," she went on. "And we got a lawyer, and we think we'll win eventually. But it's such a struggle. Maybe I shouldn't be telling you all this. . . ."

"I won't tell," Bessie said, "if that's what you mean." She finished her chocolate cake, just as Mamie appeared in the shop door. She was waving her sketch of the old gate.

"You know, I should have brought my camera!" Bessie said. "And I forgot it."

"Take it everywhere you go," Lydia said.

"I will from now on," Bessie said.

They left to go pick up the new American.

THE next morning Bessie got up early and scrambled down the ladder while Marie-Claude was still asleep.

Lydia and Philippe were just coming out of their room. It had taken Bessie a while to catch on that Lydia and Philippe were living together and weren't married. Lots of people in Delight did that—well, not lots, but her Uncle Pete had gotten divorced and lived with his girl friend. Her mother had gulped and invited them to dinner. What her mother would say about Lydia and Philippe, Bessie could not imagine.

"Want to go with me to get the milk?" Lydia asked in French. Bessie trotted along with her. Lydia carried an empty wine bottle for the milk.

Bessie looked around Mme Poulet's kitchen and liked it. There was a wood stove as well as the fireplace, and it seemed very cozy with its low-beamed ceiling and comfortable chairs. There was even a television set.

Philippe had made the coffee when they got back, and Bessie fixed her own hot chocolate. There was nothing to it—she just took some Poulain chocolate from the box and added it to hot milk—but Lydia was pleased.

"Tu es très intelligente," she said to Bessie.

"It's easy," Bessie said.

"En français," Lydia said. "C'est facile."

"C'est facile," Bessie said agreeably. She ate bread and butter while Lydia and Philippe talked about Lydia's carte de séjour. They were going into Châteauroux later to see the lawyer. But first, Philippe wanted to give Bessie a lesson in the darkroom.

Bessie was delighted. "I've always wanted to know how to develop film," she said.

"En français," Lydia said.

"Je suis heureuse," Bessie said. That meant "I am happy." In French, she had come to realize, she could say only the simplest things—but most of the time, the simplest phrase was enough to get the idea across.

Philippe tore open an unused cannister of film so he could show her how to put the film on the reel so it could be developed. She would have to load the reel in total darkness, so she had to practice with the dummy film over and over.

When she thought she had it down pat, Philippe took her into the darkroom and showed her where to place the reel on the worktable and where to put the tank.

With Lydia translating, he explained that once the film was on the reel and in the tank, with the lid on, then she could turn on the light and add the chemicals to the tank.

Philippe asked her if she was ready, and she said, "Oui." He turned off the light. Bessie had never seen anything as dark as the darkroom in her life. She opened the cannister of her film and pulled out the film, threw away the paper, threaded the film on the reel, and began to turn it slowly, carefully, until all the film was wound up on the reel. Then she put the reel in the little tank and put the lid on the tank.

"Fini," she said.

"Bon," said Philippe, and turned the light on.

The next part was complicated, but at least you could see what you were doing. You had to get all the chemicals to twenty degrees—which Bessie thought was very cold indeed until she realized that Philippe was talking about centigrade.

And each chemical had to stay in the tank a precise amount of time. This made it twice as hard for Bessie to remember, because she had to think *seven* when Philippe said "sept minutes," and then remember the length of time.

"Le temps et la température, c'est tout," Philippe said over and over. Time and temperature are everything.

Philippe mixed some developer and it was too cool. He had to get some hot water from the kitchen and set the beaker of developer in the hot water until the temperature got up to twenty degrees. Then he poured the developer in the tank and left it for seven minutes. Then he poured it out, poured in the stop bath, poured that out, and then added the fixer. Then the negatives had to be rinsed in water.

Philippe held the negatives up and looked at them. "Très bons," he said. Very good.

Bessie peered at the negatives and couldn't see much. She had never really looked at negatives before, and it was weird. There was the Eiffel Tower, not standing up quite straight. There were the rabbits and Gabrielle. What was white in real life was black in the negatives, so that Gabrielle's face was black in the negative, her hair white.

Philippe said he'd print one to show her how that was done. He put the negative in the enlarger—the agrandisseur, he called it—and explained this could be done with the safe light on. He focused. Then he made a test strip, then put photographic paper in the enlarger, timed it, dropped the paper in a pan of developer, and Bessie watched while—as if by magic—a picture appeared. It was little Gabrielle.

"Le temps," Philippe said. "Le temps." You had to time the prints, too, in the developer, in the stop bath, and in the fixer. Then you had to wash the prints in water. It was too complicated, Bessie thought.

But she was enchanted with the big print of Gabrielle.

"I'm learning photography!" she said. "I can't wait until I tell old Clark Haynes. He's the photographer at the *Delight Daily Enterprise*. He never would teach me. And I'm learning it in French. I bet he doesn't know that a negative is a *cliché* and film is *pellicule*."

Lydia laughed, and then she and Philippe set out for Châteauroux and the lawyer.

"I hate to leave Dottie just when she got here," Lydia said. Dottie was the new American who had arrived the night before. "But we've got to see about these things. You know, I feel as though I'm fighting for my life."

"It will be okay," Bessie said. "We'll all help her. Mamie's here, and Marie-Claude."

"I don't know about Dottie," Lydia said. She had her doubts about Dottie, she said. Dottie was a graduate student in English at Rutgers. She had seemed dazed when they had picked her up at Argenton. Her flight had been delayed leaving Kennedy, and she had had to land in Düsseldorf and sit there on the plane before it was allowed to go on to Paris. By the time she got to Argenton, she had been without sleep for what seemed like days.

Lydia and Philippe left, and Bessie piled the breakfast dishes in the sink and washed them. (All the guests were supposed to help with the housework at La Valette.) There weren't many dishes—just three cups— so it wasn't any big deal, but it made Bessie feel virtuous.

She took her camera and went outside, eager to photograph the world. Thierry came along with his fishing pole, and she took his picture. He was obviously pleased and said something in French which Bessie was able, after several repetitions, to understand was an invitation to go fishing with him.

"D'accord," she said. "Où?"

"Au lavoir," Thierry said. "Attends."

Obediently, Bessie waited while he ran back to his house and came out with a second fishing pole.

"Merci," she said.

The lavoir turned out to be the village laundry. Nobody used it for that anymore—except Lydia, who washed her blue jeans there—but the women in the village used to come out and do their washing there, kneeling on the side and scrubbing clothes and linens with a heavy brush on the concrete banks. There were small fish in the lavoir—Bessie could see them swimming around among the weeds in the green water.

"Regarde," said Thierry suddenly. "Regarde." He

pointed with his pole to a particularly dark green spot, and Bessie saw what at first looked like a shadow. As it moved, she saw it was a very large fish.

Thierry muttered something which Bessie didn't understand.

"Il est grand," she said. He's big.

"Magnifique!" said Thierry.

Thierry had brought bait, and Bessie put a worm on her hook and dropped it in the water. Nothing happened. Thierry was intent and silent, staring at the water. Bessie looked around at the trees and watched the birds. She had never cared much for fishing, because you didn't *do* anything when you fished. Bessie preferred more action and more plot to things she did.

She put down her pole and took some pictures of Thierry fishing.

She picked up her pole again. Fishing was very boring. She tried to figure out how to quit and go home. She couldn't. She sat down and held the pole and thought about Lydia and Philippe and Malignon and the little house at La Valette.

I have to think of something to do to help, she thought.

Finally, when she decided enough time had gone by for politeness' sake, she put her pole down and got up. "Merci," she said to Thierry. "I have to go now."

Thierry did not seem hurt or bothered in the least. In fact, she didn't think he noticed.

When she got back home, everybody else was up. Marie-Claude and Mamie and Dottie sat around the table, and Dottie still seemed dazed.

The three of them were carrying on a halting conversation in French. When Marie-Claude said something, neither Dottie nor Mamie could understand it. Marie-Claude repeated everything two or three times until they understood it.

Bessie, to her astonishment, discovered she understood Marie-Claude as well as or better than Mamie and Dottie could.

Finally, she decided that nobody was saying anything interesting enough to make it worth all that effort to figure out what it was.

She was glad when she heard a truck drive up, making a great racket with its odd-sounding horn. She went outside, and so did everybody else.

The driver got out and lowered panels on one side. Inside were racks of meat. It was a traveling butcher shop.

All the women in the village clustered around the truck, greeting the driver and making jokes. Bessie took pictures of Mme Poulet buying some sausage. Mme Brodeau, Gabrielle's mother, bought some pâté, and Marie-Claude bought a pork roast.

The truck left, and Marie-Claude asked Bessie if she'd go into Delle to get the bread and wine.

"They won't sell wine to me," Bessie said. "I'm a minor." She put it in French: "je suis trop jeune." I am too young. But Marie-Claude said in France no one was too young to buy wine.

"D'accord," Bessie said. She took the money from Marie-Claude and set out, with her camera, on a bicycle.

She pedaled out to the paved road, passed the lavoir, where Thierry was still fishing, and went into Delle. She stopped at the boulangerie, propped her bicycle against the wall, and went in.

She was about to ask for bread when she remembered.

"Bonjour, madame," she said to the woman behind the counter.

"Bonjour, mademoiselle," the woman said, smiling.

And, feeling very French, Bessie bought the bread.

She held up her camera and, in pantomime, asked permission to take the woman's picture. The woman smiled and Bessie gestured to her to hold out the bread as though she were selling it. Bessie took a flash picture of her.

Bessie put the bread in her bicycle basket and went next door for the wine, which she put in the box on the back. When she got on her bike, the wine felt a little heavy, but not too heavy, she decided.

She started to turn around to go home, and then kept going. She'd coast down the hill and go home the way Marie-Claude had shown her.

She went flying down the hill, through the cluster of little houses at the foot, and turned to the left.

SHE came to a crossroads. There were no signposts. She hesitated, turned to the right.

She pedaled along and saw nothing that looked familiar. Nothing at all. She went past lots of little fields with hedges around them. She went through a small forest that she'd never seen before. Roads turned off her road, and there were signposts pointing to towns she'd never heard of. None of them said La Valette or Delle, or even Couronne. Should she turn around and go back to Delle? Could she even find Delle now?

She kept on pedaling, and finally she met an old man with a herd of goats.

She stopped her bicycle and waited for him. She was phrasing her question, "Où est La Valette?" in her mind when he spoke to her.

"Bonjour, mademoiselle," he said, and smiled and bowed.

Of course. Everybody spoke to everybody else before they got down to business.

"Bonjour, monsieur," she said, and he smiled and nodded. And she asked, "Où est La Valette?"

She heard a torrent of French. The old man finished and looked at her expectantly. She didn't have the least idea what he had said. For a minute, she was afraid, really afraid. She was lost. And could she understand enough French to get un-lost?

Because she didn't know what else to do, she put the question again: "Où est La Valette?"

Again there was a storm of impenetrable French, but this time the old man pointed. He pointed back the way she had come and said distinctly, "A gauche."

Bessie knew that meant to the left, so she should turn around and go back and turn to the left. After that, she did not know what she should do, but she could do that much and then ask somebody else.

"Merci," she said to the old man and turned her bicycle, heavy with the wine, around and started back the way she had come.

When she came to the first crossroads, she turned to the left. She pedaled through a forest—was it the same one she'd been through earlier?—and came out in the open.

And then she saw the castle.

She saw the towers first, the tops of round towers with cone-shaped roofs, like the towers of castles in fairy-tale books. She thought for a minute that she was dreaming, and then she thought she must be really lost, lost in time as well as in space, and in a fairy-tale world.

But that is perfectly ridiculous, Bessie Hightower told herself. I don't have to pinch myself, she thought. This is France, and that's a French castle.

As she got closer she could see that the castle was very real and very substantial. She stopped in front of the big iron gates, which were padlocked, and looked up at the castle. It sprawled every which way, with towers sticking up at corners and bay windows jutting out at odd angles. It looked like someone's dream castle, but it was real. There was an old man sitting on a bench in the sun, by a wall of the castle. There was a chapel at one corner of the castle.

She got out her camera and took several pictures.

She pedaled on, feeling very lost.

Then she saw the little church. It was a tiny one-room chapel right by the side of the road. Bessie stopped and got off her bicycle and went over to it. It seemed so strange, out there all by itself. It was a very funny little building—it must be very old. It reminded her of Saint-Benoît-du-Sault. She took a picture of it.

She tried the door, but it was locked. She looked in a window and saw a few wooden benches scattered about, not standing in neat rows. There was a little altar, and a window above it and niches on either side of the window. In one niche was a carved wooden statue; the other niche was empty. The wooden statue that belonged there was lying on the floor. It looked very old and very dusty.

The wooden statue in the niche was not like anything she had ever seen. It was a woman carved with great energy and strength—and the woman held a baby, and the baby was laughing up at the woman. Bessie liked them both very much.

She decided to try to take a flash picture of the statue through the window. She didn't know how it would come out, but it seemed worth a try.

After taking the picture, she sat on the steps of the little church a minute, and then, sighing, got back on her bicycle and started off again. I wish I knew where I am, she thought. But I can't be too far away. After all, I got here on a bicycle, so I can get home on a bicycle. Unless I *am* in a time and space warp. . . .

Before she could pursue that possibility, she came to a cluster of little houses, and there was a woman working in the vegetable garden of one of the houses.

"Bonjour, madame," Bessie said, stopping.

The woman straightened up. "Bonjour, mademoiselle."

"Où est La Valette?" asked Bessie.

This time Bessie recognized the phrase "à droite," which stood out like a diamond in the midst of all the other French. That meant to the right.

Hot dog, she thought. "Merci," she said. She pedaled on.

She turned right at the next crossroads and then went on to the next crossroads. There was a signpost that said La Valette, and it pointed to the right.

La Valette was just past the crossroads.

And there she was, home again, and there was Marie-Claude in the vegetable garden.

"I got lost," Bessie said. "I found a little church and a castle!"

Marie-Claude, of course, didn't understand, but Bessie *had* to tell her. She took the bread and wine inside, and got her dictionary, and said, "J'étais perdue" (I was lost) "et j'ai trouvé un château et une petite église" (and I found a castle and a little church).

Marie-Claude knew immediately which castle and church she was talking about, and scratched a map in the sand to show Bessie where she'd been. The château, she said, was "une maison particulière," a private home, where a family of old nobility still lived.

When Lydia and Philippe got back from the lawyer's office, they, too, had to hear about Bessie's adventure. Lydia said there were other castles like that which were open to the public, and they'd take Bessie and the others to see some of them. The little chapel, Philippe said, was abandoned. It had belonged to a village that had once existed outside the castle gates.

Mamie and Dottie were both tired and went to bed early that night—but Bessie stayed up to talk to Philippe and Lydia. They talked about castles and their visit to the lawyer.

Bessie felt like the old hand at La Valette now.

"Don't tell Mamie and Dottie about all this trouble with Malignon," Lydia said. "I don't want to worry them."

"Are any other Americans coming for July?" Bessie asked.

"Yes," Lydia said. "Two young men. They should be here any day now."

"What will you do if we have to move out?" Bessie asked.

"I don't have the faintest idea," Lydia said. "We *can't* have to move out."

Lydia and Philippe had lots of work to do, getting up the information for the impôt people. "I thought I'd kept good financial records," Lydia said. "Now I don't know."

They weren't sure what they'd have to do about Lydia's carte de séjour. You just couldn't stay on and on in France. Lydia had indeed gone back to the United States that spring, as Bessie knew, but her passport had not been stamped when she came back to France, so the authorities were questioning that she had really left.

"I might just have to take the train and go to Luxembourg," Lydia said. "Stay overnight and come back."

"Quelle histoire," Bessie said.

Dottie chose pottery for her programme de travail, and Philippe gave her a lesson on the potter's wheel in the shed the next morning.

Dottie giggled when she felt the clay ooze through her fingers as she held it on the wheel. She did not seem very adept at potting, but Bessie took her picture at the potter's wheel.

Then she took a picture of Mamie, who was sketching the rabbit cages.

Bessie went inside to change her film, and sat down at the dining table, where Lydia was again working on the income tax papers.

"Mon Dieu!" groaned Lydia. Bessie shook her head in sympathy, and put more film in her Instamatic. She was dying to develop her film—the pictures of the castle and the church and Thierry should be a lot better than the ones of the rabbits and Gabrielle.

Philippe was happy to avoid the impôts papers, and came in the darkroom and showed her how to mix the chemicals herself. Then he got out the little reel and the tank and told her to turn out the light and go ahead.

Feeling more expert this time, Bessie opened the cannister of film, threaded it on the reel, and wound it. Once the reel was safely in the tank, she turned on the light and did everything just as Philippe had told her—developer, stop bath, and fixer.

Then she rinsed the negatives in water and lifted them up to look at them.

"Philippe!" she called.

Philippe came in and peered at the long strip of negatives.

"Quelle histoire," he said.

"Qu'est-ce que c'est?" Bessie asked. What is it?

There were white spots all over her negatives, and Philippe explained it was because she hadn't loaded the film on the reel properly. All the film had not been exposed to the developer.

Were the pictures a total loss? she asked. "Est-ce que tout est perdu?"

They were, Philippe said, a total loss. All ruined.

Lydia tried to console Bessie. "Tout le monde se trompe parfois," she said. Everybody makes mistakes.

But that did not cheer Bessie Hightower. "All my lovely pictures," she mourned. "Thierry fishing. The woman at the boulangerie. Dottie at the potter's wheel. The château. The little church."

Lydia pointed out she could reshoot all of those quite easily.

"Oh, well," said Bessie, "my mother always says, 'We learn by our mistakes.' "

Philippe patted her on the head and went back to the dining table and the impôts papers.

Marie-Claude gathered up the three Americans and suggested they go to Delle.

They met the old woman with the geese again, and

Mamie, of course, was carried away by how picturesque, how charming, she was. Bessie took the old woman's picture.

In Delle they went to the post office, where Bessie mailed the letter she'd written the day she got there—it seemed like years ago—and watched the postman weigh it on a little brass scale. They all bought picture postcards at the café and sat down and had drinks. Bessie had warm orange soda and thought, I might even get to like this stuff.

When they went shopping, Bessie took another flash picture of the woman in the boulangerie. They watched Marie-Claude buy wine and cheese and rice.

Dottie wanted to cash a traveler's check, but Delle had no bank. Mamie wanted to buy a zipper to repair a skirt, so Marie-Claude said they'd have to get Philippe or Lydia to take them to Couronne that afternoon.

Couronne was bigger than Delle and almost as old as Saint-Benoît-du-Sault. It had narrow little winding streets and dozens of shops and cafés.

Philippe drove to a filling station where he wanted to have some work done on the car. Marie-Claude took Mamie and Dottie to the bank.

Lydia said she wanted to buy a new bicycle pump—did Bessie want to come with her?

"Certainement," Bessie said.

They walked past the church—which was very old, Lydia said—and past the halle, the old public market, and then they turned down a side street.

"There," said Lydia, "across the street. Those are Malignon's shops."

Bessie looked and saw a shop that said ANTIQUAIRE in big letters on the window. Next to the antique shop was a gift shop with lots of gray pottery in one window.

61

"He makes those dishes at his pottery outside Couronne," Lydia said.

"Let's go look at his stuff," Bessie said.

"No, no," Lydia said. "I don't want him to see us. I usually don't even go down this street when I come to Couronne."

"But why?" Bessie said. "You shouldn't be afraid of him."

"I'm not afraid," Lydia said. "I just don't want to have any trouble with him."

"Too bad," Bessie said. "I like antique shops. My mother likes antiques, and she's always dragged me into junk shops all my life. The best things are always in the back room."

"Tell me about your family, Bessie," Lydia said.

"I have two brothers—one is eight and one is six," she said. "Sam is eight and Dan is six. Sam's whole name is Sam Houston Hightower. Dan's going to start school this fall, and my mother wants to start a plant-and-antique shop downtown when he does. My father said he thought life was more fun before women started to want to be fulfilled."

"And what did your mother say to that?" Lydia asked.

"She said she was fulfilled enough, thank you, but she just wanted to get out of the house."

"Have you always lived in Texas?" Lydia asked.

"I'm a sixth-generation Texan," Bessie said. "Both my father and my mother and all my grandparents were born in Texas."

"My goodness," Lydia said, "maybe you'll be the one to get to do something different."

Bessie thought about this while Lydia bought the bicycle pump.

They all met, as arranged, at a sidewalk café, and Bessie, at Lydia's suggestion, ordered a citron pressé, which is what the French call lemonade. (A limonade, Bessie was to learn, was a lemon soda.) While they waited, Bessie took a picture of everyone sitting around the table under the umbrella.

The citron pressé had ice in it, and Bessie was in seventh heaven. "J'adore Couronne," she said.

When the car was ready, they all drove down to see some castle ruins at Couronne-Dessous.

Bessie strolled along behind Philippe and Lydia and the others as they walked down the road where they had parked. She looked up at the castle, or what was left of it. The wall had fallen down in places, but the portal where the outside gate had been was still there.

Philippe, who seemed to know an awful lot about castles, was explaining about the gates, but Bessie couldn't understand what he was saying.

She walked through a second portal and into the courtyard of the castle.

She loved it. The wall stretched all the way around to form an enormous rectangle. In some places, the wall was still high and strong and ornamented with parapets and crenelations and towers. Where it had tumbled down, the gaps were covered with vines. Inside the courtyard, weeds and trees had grown up.

But somehow, Bessie liked it *because* it was a ruin, the shadow of a castle. It was more romantic and mysterious even than the whole, lovely, well-kept castle with the pointed top towers she had seen the day she got lost. You could imagine a castle better the way it had been in the beginning, she thought, if it wasn't all there.

Near the gate, there were some buildings that had

partly tumbled down. One looked as though it might have been a little church. Over in another corner was another little building that was even more of a mess.

Bessie stood in a patch of clover, looking around, turning slowly, taking it all in, noticing the stonework, the narrow windows, the ledges, everything that was left.

She ran over to the churchlike building near the gate and went inside and looked up. The roof was gone, but some of the walls were still standing, and they were very high. You could see niches in the walls, some of them very high up.

She went out and around that building to a big tower in the corner of the wall. Inside the tower was a crumbling circular stone stairway. She climbed up it as far as she could, and looked out a tiny slit of a window. She marveled at the way the men who had built the stairway had used big, heavy stones. The treads of the stairs had been made of wedge-shaped stones, and they went around and around, with the narrow ends of the wedges stacked in the middle and the wide ends anchored in the stone walls of the round tower.

She left the tower, went over to the other side of the gate, and explored all the nooks and crannies and passageways that still stood. She climbed up walls, crawled through underbrush, jumped, by mistake, into stinging nettles, leaped across chasms where walls had fallen down.

Then she tried to follow the big wall around the courtyard, which was bigger than two or three city blocks.

"Bess-ee!" She heard Lydia calling and went back to the others.

"How old is it?" Bessie asked.

Philippe looked blank.

"Quel âge a-t-il?" she asked.

Philippe told her it was built in the eleventh century.

"L'église?" she asked, pulling Philippe's arm and pointing to the building she thought might be a church.

"Non," Philippe said. "Donjon."

Bessie thought he meant dungeon, and was about to ask him a question about prisoners when she heard Lydia explaining to the others that *donjon* sounded like *dungeon,* but was the tower where the lord of the castle lived. (A prison was called an oubliette.)

"But it looks like a church," Bessie said, pointing to the building's windows, which had pointed arches.

Philippe explained, with Lydia helping out, that castles had had pointed arches, too. The niches were where fireplaces had been, and there had been fireplaces on the second and third floors, proving that it was a residence, not a chapel.

Everybody was ready to go, but they waited while Bessie took pictures of everything.

All the way home, Bessie asked Philippe questions about castles, working away in French. Philippe answered her patiently. Bessie understood lots of it.

When they drove up to La Valette, Mme Poulet and Joseph and Jacques and Mme Brodeau and Thierry and his mother, Mme Guitry, were all standing out in front of Lydia's house.

They piled out of the car to find out what was the matter.

Malignon had been there.

M. Malignon himself had come, driving the old lady

65

who owned the house, his old nurse. They had knocked on the door, found no one at home, and had opened the door and gone in.

Lydia exclaimed in outrage. Philippe muttered. Marie-Claude frowned.

Mme Poulet clucked. Mme Brodeau patted Lydia on the shoulder. Jacques clapped Philippe on the back encouragingly. Gabrielle laughed. Thierry muttered, "Mauvais. Mauvais."

"What?" cried Mamie. "What is it?"

"It's against the law!" Lydia cried in English. "It's trespassing. Even though she owns the house, she can't go in it while we have a lease! I'm going over to Mme Poulet's house to call the lawyer and get an injunction!"

"What is going on?" said Dottie.

"Will somebody please explain to us?" said Mamie.

Lydia at last took Mamie and Dottie into the dining room, sat down at the dining table, and explained the whole situation to them.

"We're right and he's wrong," Lydia said when she'd finished explaining about Malignon. "Our lawyer says he can't get us evicted. But it takes time to get things done in France. Oh, I have to go use the phone." She ran off.

"This is awful," Dottie said. "I don't want to stay if there's going to be trouble."

"It certainly is an *unpleasant* situation," Mamie said.

"Oh, for heaven's sake, nothing's happened yet," Bessie said.

But Dottie was upset, and Mamie wasn't too happy about it.

When Lydia came back, she reported that Mme Poulet had just received a call for her. The two young

American men had arrived. They were going to catch the bus from Argenton to Delle and would be there at seven o'clock.

"Marie-Claude, will you and Bessie go to meet them on bicycles?" Lydia said. "Philippe and I have to go to Châteauroux right away."

Bessie said she'd be glad to.

"Tu es très gentille," Lydia said.

Bessie glowed all the way to Delle, as she and Marie-Claude rode down between the fields of sweet-smelling hay. Blackberries were growing on vines by the road, she noticed. Marie-Claude said they were called mûres.

"Where is Edouard?" Bessie asked Marie-Claude in French. "He never comes."

Marie-Claude said that he had liked Lisa.

Bessie wanted to ask about Edouard's henna, but she didn't know how to do it.

Well, it will be fun to have two American boys at La Valette, she decided.

Tʜᴇ two American boys were awful.

Bessie and Marie-Claude were waiting for the bus when it pulled up in Delle across the street from the boulangerie. Several people got off, including two young men who were wearing cutoffs and carrying backpacks.

Their names were Kevin Thomas and Don Miller.

"We had a horrible trip," Kevin said. He was bigger than Don, and they were to find that he talked more. "Icelandic Airlines lost my suitcase. We missed the train to Argenton yesterday. We finally got there, and then Lydia couldn't pick us up. She's supposed to pick us up in Argenton."

"Elle était obligée d'aller à Châteauroux," Bessie said.

"What?" Kevin said.

"She had to go to Châteauroux on business," Bessie said.

It turned out that Kevin and Don knew no French, none at all.

"Then what are you doing here?" Bessie asked. "The brochure said you had to speak French."

"I don't know," Kevin said. "We saw the ad and it seemed like a good idea."

They loaded the backpacks and Don's suitcase on the bicycles, and Bessie and Marie-Claude walked while the boys pushed the bikes.

Kevin and Don admired the countryside on the way to La Valette—Who wouldn't? thought Bessie—but when they got home and saw the house, they stood stock-still in front of it and gasped.

"You mean this is it?" Kevin said. "This is a hovel."

"Sssssh," Bessie said. "They'll hear you."

"Who?" asked Don.

"The other people in the village," Bessie said. "Marie-Claude."

"I don't care," Kevin said. "They can't understand English anyway."

Inside, Kevin and Don met Mamie and Dottie, and Marie-Claude showed them to their room, which was in the loft above the big room that Mamie and Dottie shared. "I don't think this ladder's safe," Kevin said.

Marie-Claude showed them the latrine and the outdoor shower. Kevin was shocked at the latrine. "I can't sit on that," Kevin said.

"Why not?" Bessie asked. She was genuinely curious.

"I just can't," Kevin said. "It looks awful. Oh, well, at least I brought my own toilet paper."

"I'd hate to lug toilet paper across the ocean," Bessie said.

"I'm glad I did," Kevin said. "Look at this." He picked up the French toilet paper that lay on the seat. "It's like high-grade sandpaper."

"Well, the outdoor shower is lots of fun," Bessie said. "Especially at night under the stars."

69

When Lydia and Philippe got back from Châteauroux, everyone had supper, and it was a delicious pork roast.

Kevin and Don did not want wine. Alcohol was poison, they said. They did not want hot chocolate because it had white sugar in it, and white sugar was poison, too. Tea had caffeine in it. They said they'd drink milk, until they found out the milk wasn't pasteurized.

Bessie decided she'd drink a little wine in a glass of water. Kevin and Don were so awful she wanted to be on the side of the French. She disliked them so much she wanted to *be* French.

Kevin and Don drank only water, but they ate more than their share of the pork roast. Kevin said they needed lots of protein after their journey.

Everyone was truly glad when Kevin and Don went to bed early.

Bessie decided when things quieted down that she'd try to develop some more film. Philippe encouraged her to go ahead.

She turned out the lights, opened her film, and wound it on the reel as carefully as she could. It felt right. She turned on the lights and did the chemicals, and then fearfully took out the negatives and looked at them. They looked all right. She rinsed them and wiped them off with a squeegee and hung them up to dry.

Philippe came in and said they looked great.

Bessie felt very relieved.

Philippe said he'd print one of them for her. He took the new picture of Thierry fishing and enlarged it and cropped the print. Bessie thought it was beautiful when he got through with it.

Philippe made a print of the woman in the boulangerie, and Bessie was disappointed. "It's not as good," she said.

Philippe explained that flash pictures never were. Natural light made the best pictures, he said. But her camera was so small and simple you couldn't use it without a flash except outdoors in bright sunshine. He would show her soon, he promised, how to use a more complicated camera where you could open the shutter wide and take pictures inside without a flash.

The next morning was even worse. Kevin and Don were in the kitchen when she came down the ladder.

"We're hungry," Don said.

"We've been up for hours," Kevin said. "Where's Lydia?"

"She'll be up in a minute," Bessie said. "She'll make the coffee. I'll go get the milk. Want to come with me?"

Kevin and Don trotted along behind her on the way to Mme Poulet's house. Bessie carried the wine bottle.

"You mean you get the milk in a wine bottle?" Kevin said. "That's so unsanitary."

"Nobody's died yet," Bessie said.

"Bonjour, Bess-ee," Mme Poulet said.

"Bonjour, madame," said Bessie, feeling very French. "Du lait, s'il vous plaît."

"Oui, bien sûr," Mme Poulet said.

Bessie introduced Kevin and Don, and Mme Poulet clucked when she found out they spoke no French at all.

"Vous apprendrez," she said. You will learn.

71

She handed Bessie the wine bottle full of milk and added, "Bess-ee a bien appris le français."

"Merci, madame," said Bessie, so proud she was flustered.

"What did she say?" Don asked.

"She said I had learned French well," Bessie said.

"I guess we can learn it too, then, Don," Kevin said.

"Not if you don't try," Bessie said.

When they got back, Lydia was making the coffee. She got bread and butter out, heated the milk, made Bessie's hot chocolate.

She called Philippe. Mamie and Dottie came in, and everybody sat down and began to eat. Except Kevin and Don.

"You mean this is breakfast?" Kevin said.

"C'est le petit déjeuner," Lydia said.

"What did she say?" Kevin asked Bessie.

"She said, yes, it's breakfast," Bessie said, a little bored with translating everything.

"Isn't there any orange juice?" Kevin asked.

"Sorry," Lydia said in English. "The French don't drink orange juice for breakfast."

Bessie remembered with some embarrassment that she, too, had wanted orange juice when she first came, and that she'd spit out the warm milk.

"Oh, well, we brought lots of vitamin C tablets," Kevin said. "We can take those, can't we, Don?"

Don nodded and began to eat bread.

"But I do like protein for breakfast," Kevin went on. "Can I possibly have an omelette for breakfast?"

"An omelette?" said Lydia. "For breakfast?" She translated for Marie-Claude and Philippe, who looked horrified. They were shocked, Bessie saw, that anyone would want eggs for breakfast.

Nevertheless, Lydia got up from the table and went to the tiny refrigerator. "Pas d'œufs," she said. "J'irai chez Poulet."

"What did she say?" Kevin asked.

"She said she didn't have any eggs," Bessie said, "but she'd go over to Madame Poulet's to get some."

"No eggs," said Kevin. "That's poor management."

"The French shop every day," Bessie said. "They don't keep lots of things on hand. They like fresh food."

"Everybody ought to keep eggs," Kevin said.

"Not if they don't eat them for breakfast," Bessie said.

Lydia came back and cooked Kevin an omelette. He ate it, thanked Lydia, and then opened his knapsack, in which he carried his American toilet paper, and got out several bottles of vitamin tablets. He and Don took an assortment of various pills.

"If you take all that stuff," Bessie asked, "what difference does it make whether you eat protein or not?"

"There are many nutrients that haven't been synthesized yet," Kevin said. "You have to eat as many natural foods as you can and supplement those with pills."

Kevin and Don wanted to go sightseeing. Lydia and Philippe had to go back to Châteauroux, and they offered to take anyone who wanted to go.

"What is there to see in Châteauroux?" Don asked.

There was a small museum, Lydia said, and an old house that was open to the public. There were shops, banks, and even a supermarket.

Everybody but Bessie and Marie-Claude got in the car and went off to Châteauroux.

Bessie decided to ride a bicycle to Couronne and maybe go back to the castle. Was it too far? she asked

73

Marie-Claude. (It was astonishing, she thought, how she now heard herself carrying on French conversations with Marie-Claude and Philippe.)

Marie-Claude said it was about ten kilometers, a good, stiff ride "à vélo," but certainly possible.

"That's only six miles," Bessie said. "I can do that."

She took her knapsack and put in her camera, a Michelin map that Marie-Claude found for her, and a lunch: a piece of bread, a pear, and some cheese.

It was a long way to Couronne, uphill and downhill. The downhill stretches were marvelous, but the uphill parts were a bore. She kept on, though, pumping away, and got to Couronne. She stopped at the sidewalk café and sat there sipping a citron pressé, watching the traffic, all by herself having a lovely time.

If people in Delight could only see me now, she thought. She tried to imagine what a sidewalk café would look like on Main Street in Delight.

She stopped at the charcuterie and bought a piece of sausage to upgrade her lunch, and went by the épicerie to buy some chocolate.

Then, well supplied, she started down the street. On an impulse, she turned down the side street that went past Malignon's antique shop.

She propped her bicycle up against the wall and went inside.

A tall, formidable lady with blonde hair that was dark at the roots spoke to her in a frosty voice: "Mademoiselle."

"Bonjour, madame," Bessie said.

The lady was cold and stiff. She watched Bessie closely as Bessie looked at the sets of china in a glass case, fingered an old French military uniform on a dummy, and flipped through some old postcards.

When Bessie found a postcard from Galveston, Texas, on which somebody had written a spidery message in French in 1920, and mailed it to his mother in France, she decided to buy it.

"Combien?" she asked, holding it up. How much?

"Honk-honk," said the lady.

"Combien?" Bessie asked again.

"Trois francs," said the lady, holding up three fingers.

"Bien," said Bessie, who thought that was very high. But she got out her money and gave the lady three francs.

"Merci, mademoiselle," the lady said.

"Je viens de Texas," Bessie said. I come from Texas. She pointed at the postcard.

The lady bowed her head slightly, but said nothing. She looked as though she couldn't have cared less. Bessie, rebuffed, moved through the room again, and headed toward the back room out of long habit.

The antique shop wasn't too different from American antique shops. In fact, it was more like an American antique shop than anything else in France was like anything else in America. So . . . there had to be a back room.

Bessie sailed through a door and into the back room. Just as she had expected, it was full of furniture that needed repairing, teapots without lids, unmatched goblets, and other treasures like the things Bessie's mother had been buying for as long as Bessie could remember.

Someone else came in the front door, and the blonde lady turned back to answer the newcomer's questions.

Bessie moved through this second room because she saw another door. Through the door, in the dim light of the third room, she saw more treasures—some old cornices, broken columns, two old doors, two shutters—and two statutes.

They were very old and carved of wood, and one was a mother holding a baby, and the baby was looking up at his mother and laughing.

They were just like the statues from the little church she'd seen the day she got lost coming home from Delle. She was staring at them with delight when she felt a hand on her shoulder.

"Mademoiselle!" said the blonde woman. "Viens ici. Cette chambre n'est pas ouverte au public." Come here. This room is not open.

Bessie shook off the woman's hand, but the woman grabbed her by the arm and pulled her back to the front of the shop.

"Je m'excuse," Bessie said. "Je regrette que . . ."

"Certainement," said the woman. She added that the back rooms were private. Customers were permitted only in the front room. Was there something else mademoiselle desired? Some question she would like to pose? If not . . .

Bessie decided it was time to leave.

"Au revoir, madame," she said.

"Au revoir," the woman said coldly.

Outside, Bessie put her postcard in her knapsack and got on the bicycle and pedaled away. She rode down the hill to Couronne-Dessous and pushed her bicycle up the last hill to the castle. She walked in the courtyard and sat down in a patch of clover and thought hard.

Were those the same statues she'd seen in the little chapel? Did that mean Malignon was a thief?

76

What she should do, she realized, was to take a picture of the statues in the antique shop.

But how could she do that?

Could she just go back to the shop and say she wanted to take a picture? Somehow, Bessie felt that was not a good idea.

She pulled out her bread and cheese and sausage and ate while she thought. She ate the pear, and then she ate the chocolate. She thought hard.

She looked around the castle, at the walls and the donjon, and tried to imagine it when a thousand people lived within its walls. What would those people have done about Malignon? They would have sent a knight in armor to knock him off, that's what they would have done. Lydia would have been a lady in distress, who needed help. Philippe was great, Bessie thought hastily, but he was more the artistic type— good at weaving, pottery, photography, and drawing. The two of them needed a knight, all right.

Then troubadours could make up a song to sing in the great hall of the donjon at night, about the downfall of the wicked Malignon.

But back to the present . . . Bessie thought. It would have to be Bessie and a camera on a bicycle, instead of a knight on horseback with a lance.

Maybe she could bring somebody with her to talk to the woman in the antique shop while she slipped back and got a picture. Would Marie-Claude do it? She'd be good, because she could talk French to the blonde lady. What about Mamie? She could be the big American tourist lady, and maybe that would interest the blonde.

But somehow, Bessie did not want to bring grown people into this. Grown people had a way of screwing

77

things up. They either squelched interesting plots and schemes, or they took everything over and did it their own way. The best thing by far, Bessie thought, was to act on her own.

She got on her bicycle and started back to Couronne. She stopped at the café again and had another citron pressé with beaucoup de glace. Lots of ice.

The ice must have made her brain work, she decided. Because she realized the back room must have a back door.

She got on her bicycle and rode down the street in front of Malignon's shop.

The blonde lady had her back to the front door when Bessie went by. Bessie turned sharply at the next corner and went back up toward the center of town, looking for an alley or passageway that would lead her to the back of Malignon's shop. And she found a passageway immediately. It led to another passage between buildings that ended up right behind what must be the antique shop and the gift shop.

In fact, there was a parked truck that had *Poterie Malignon* lettered on it.

And there was a little door that must lead into the antique-shop side. Bessie stopped some distance away from the shop, got off her bike, took her camera out of her knapsack, made sure there was film in it, made sure the flashcube was new, made sure everything was set. She ran to the door. It was locked. It was as tight as a bank vault.

But there was a little open window next to it. She looked in the window and she could see the statues, but they were over by the door to the shop's middle room, and she was afraid they were much too far away to get a decent picture.

She took one anyway.

And then she decided to climb in the window and go get a better picture. She prayed the big blonde woman was busy in the front room.

She held the camera strap in her teeth and threw one leg over the window, then the other. She jumped to the floor and ran over and quickly got a picture of the statues.

She was just barely out the window when she heard the woman shouting at her. She didn't dare look back. She picked up her bike and pedaled for dear life.

WHEN she got home, Mamie was standing around the yard. "I wish I had a chair," she said. "There's no place to sit down here." It seemed she had sketched everything she could draw from where she had sat on the stone steps that led to the vegetable garden, and there really wasn't anyplace else to sit.

"Bring a chair from inside," Bessie suggested.

"There aren't any chairs inside," Mamie said. "Just benches at the table." She looked disconsolate.

"Where's everybody else?" Bessie asked.

"Dottie's lying down. Kevin and Don are lying down. The others are in the dining room."

Bessie found Lydia and Philippe and Marie-Claude deep in conference around the table. They looked up when she came in. "Ça va," they said.

"Ça va," Bessie said. "What's the matter?" Everyone did look worried.

"Same old thing," Lydia said. "Same old problems. The French law is so different from American law. Everything works slowly. Malignon has so much influence that sometimes I think even our lawyer is in awe of him. I don't know. . . ."

Bessie was dying to tell them about the statues in Malignon's shop. But she didn't. There were several reasons. For one thing, she wasn't sure it was important. They all looked so worried. She was reluctant to tell anything to grown people, and while Philippe and Lydia were just barely grown up, they were grown up. And then, she had gone to Malignon's shop when Lydia had told her not to.

Lydia was still talking about their troubles, and she had a new one. Don and Kevin were causing a great deal of vexation because they knew no French at all, because they complained all the time, because their dietary requirements were a real bore. What could be done to get them to settle down and accept life at La Valette and learn some French? They all discussed this—but no one had a solution.

Mamie came in and said that Dottie was crying in their room and couldn't stop. Lydia sighed and said she'd go talk to her.

Lydia came back and reported that Dottie was very unhappy. Things hadn't gone well at school that semester—in fact, Dottie wasn't going back to finish graduate school. And now she was disappointed in her French vacation. She wasn't learning French, and Don and Kevin annoyed her. She didn't feel a part of things, either.

"And while I was in there talking to Dottie," Lydia said, "I could hear Kevin and Don upstairs grumbling and complaining, and Kevin moaned, 'Oh, how did we end up here?' "

Lydia was almost in tears. "Everything's falling apart because Philippe and I have to spend all our time going to the lawyers because of that monster, Malignon," she said.

She began to cry, while Mamie and Marie-Claude and Philippe and Bessie stared at her, helpless.

Then Lydia looked up, dried her eyes on her shirt-tail, and announced, "I'm going to see Jules."

Philippe smiled, and Marie-Claude shrugged.

"Who is Jules?" Bessie asked.

"Jules est sorcier," Philippe said.

"Sorcier?" asked Bessie.

A sorcier, it seems, was a sorcerer. And Jules was supposed to be a sorcerer. He lived a couple of villages away, and all the French people were fond of him.

"Bessie, come with me," Lydia said. "He'd love to meet you."

A sorcerer? That was absurd, Bessie thought. But she said, "Sure, I'll go—even if I *am* so tired I probably can't pedal ten more feet."

They rode bicycles up the road toward the place where Jules lived.

"Is he really a sorcerer?" Bessie asked. "Spells and all that?"

"Oh, who knows," Lydia said. "The village people call him a sorcerer. This part of France—the Berry—is the only part where sorcerers are supposed to still be around. I don't know whether it's magic or not, but he's a wonderful old character. He was a prisoner during World War II—like Jacques and Joseph—and he's never married. He lives by himself with his dog and his goat."

Bessie had a number of things she wanted to ask Lydia. She wanted to ask her why she and Philippe didn't get married—they obviously loved each other very much. They never quarreled or spoke crossly to one another. But she didn't ask her that.

She did ask her about Marie-Claude. Who was she?

82

What was she going to do? "The first day I was here, I thought she was a kind of servant," Bessie said.

"Oh, no," Lydia said. "She's an old friend of Philippe's and Edouard's. They were all at the lycée together."

"But Edouard liked Lisa," Bessie said.

"Not really," Lydia said. "He really likes Marie-Claude, but she says she doesn't want to be tied down to him. So he used to come over to see Lisa—that was his excuse. He doesn't come as much anymore."

Bessie put all this in her pipe to smoke it, as her grandfather would have said.

Jules was at home, and he was very old, just as Lydia had said. He was delighted to see them, and patted Bessie's red hair and called her Mignonne and invited them in. He gave Lydia a glass of wine and Bessie a glass of water with one drop of wine in it to color it pink.

He talked to Lydia at some length in French that Bessie was disappointed to realize she couldn't understand at all. It didn't sound like any French she'd ever heard.

Then Lydia talked to Jules. She told him about Kevin and Don. And Dottie. And the impôt, the carte de séjour, the visit of Malignon to the house while they were gone. He seemed to know, already, about some of these things, but he listened attentively.

Then he started talking again, and Bessie's attention wandered. She patted the dog, a huge, big, black dog, who lay between her and Jules. They were sitting around a table in front of a fireplace. On the mantel were pictures of people in very old-fashioned clothes. And on the wall was a calendar that was, Bessie noticed with astonishment, thirty years old. There were stacks of newspapers that were so old they were brown. There was very little else in the room, which was small and low-ceilinged. The door was open, and Bessie could see the goat outside and a grove of trees around a little pond. It was very quiet and peaceful here, and she almost went off to sleep while Jules talked.

At last, Lydia got up to go. She thanked Jules, and he shrugged. He patted Bessie's head again and told her she was beautiful. Bessie could only smile at him.

"Well, what did he say?" Bessie asked. "I couldn't understand one word he said."

"He has a strong Berrichon accent," Lydia said. "He said to take everybody out to dinner. He said maybe that would loosen everybody up and make everybody feel part of a group."

"Are you going to do that?" Bessie asked.

"I think we will," Lydia said. "We can go up to Malicornay and have a nice meal at that little restaurant up there."

The whole group went up to Malicornay and ate dinner at a long table in a room that was like a big porch. The food was marvelous, and the service was wonderful. Everybody did seem to relax and enjoy the dinner. There was plenty of protein for Kevin and Don, and no white sugar. They drank water, as did Bessie. Everybody else drank lots of wine and became very, very cheerful.

The next morning, without comment, Lydia cooked an omelette for Kevin and Don. The others, fiercely proud, ate bread and butter and jam, and sipped hot coffee with milk or, in Bessie's case, hot chocolate.

Lydia said she and Philippe really needed to go back to Châteauroux.

"Would all of you work on your projects today?" she

asked. "We can go sightseeing tomorrow . . . maybe to George Sand's house."

Bessie was delighted. She wanted to develop the picture of the statues anyway.

Mamie said certainly, she was always content to sketch and go for walks. Not, she added hastily, that she wanted to miss a trip to George Sand's house, or anywhere else for that matter.

Kevin and Don, of course, didn't want to do a project. Lydia insisted. So they agreed to do some weaving. Philippe took them up to the loft and got them started on a loom.

Marie-Claude would stay with them and help them with their weaving, Lydia said, and give them a French lesson at the same time.

Dottie went out to the potter's wheel, and Mamie picked up her sketchbook.

Bessie was very careful in the darkroom, and when she was through developing, she sighed with relief when she saw the negatives.

There were the statues, as clear as anything. She'd let the negatives dry properly, she decided, and then she'd get Philippe to help her print them.

Now she wanted to go back and see if the statues were still in the chapel. And I can get another picture of the chapel and the château, she thought.

She went outside and saw old Mamie drawing away.

"Mamie, would you like to ride bikes with me and go see that castle I found the time I got lost?" she asked.

"I sure would," Mamie said. "But how can we find it?"

"We can go to Delle and get lost," Bessie said. "I think I know what I did."

"Let's ask Marie-Claude," said Mamie, who was more

cautious. Once a mother, always a mother, thought Bessie. But then, maybe Mamie was right. Getting lost wasn't all that much fun.

Marie-Claude drew them a map on a piece of paper and suggested they take a lunch.

With the map, they found the castle without any trouble, and Mamie sat right down on the ground in front of the gates and began to draw it.

Bessie took pictures of it and then went up the road to the chapel. She peered in the window.

The statues were gone.

So. Well, that proved the statues were in Malignon's shop. He's a thief, thought Bessie. A real thief. He stole the statues. That's good—all we have to do is expose him, and then Lydia and Philippe will be safe.

She went around to the front door of the chapel and tried it. It was still locked. She tried the windows and found one that was open. It was simple. Somebody had gone in through the window and stolen the statues.

Well, now, she thought, walking back down the road to the castle. . . . What does it all mean?

WHAT did it all mean?

She and Mamie ate their bread and cheese sitting on the grass by the road near the castle gates. Mamie said she'd come back another day and draw the chapel. She wanted to do another sketch of the castle, and then she'd be ready to go.

Waiting for Mamie, Bessie went back to the chapel and went in through the open window. She liked the little stone-floored building very much. It was an ideal church, she decided, small and symmetrical. Except for those hard wooden benches without backs. That would make it hard to sit through a sermon.

She climbed out the window and went back to the castle and waited for Mamie. Then they pedaled home, slowly.

"Look at the wild flowers," Mamie said. Only, of course, she said, "Regarde les fleurs sauvages."

"Oui," said Bessie, thinking about the statues in Malignon's shop.

"Do you find to be here is amusing?" Mamie asked her.

"Oui," said Bessie, "et vous?"

Mamie answered slowly, using English words when she didn't know enough French. "Yes, it's amusing, but there are problems. There isn't any place to sit down, you know. And I don't have a bed lamp, so I can't read in bed. I can't read anywhere at all, for that matter."

"Who wants to read?" asked Bessie. "I don't have time."

"And it's all so disorganized," Mamie said. "I know Lydia and Philippe are young, but meals are never at any certain time. You never know what's going to happen that day. I wish there were more structure."

"Have you ever been to a girls' camp?" Bessie asked.

"Well, yes, I have," Mamie said. "That was a long time ago. I loved it. I adored it."

"Well, I hate camp," Bessie said. "I don't like bugles blowing, and I don't like to get up at a certain time every day and eat breakfast at a certain time and then go do macramé. I like it here. And Lydia and Philippe are so worried about all their problems. . . ."

"You're right, Bessie," Mamie said. "I shouldn't complain. I know they're just getting started. I like them both very much. But I'm afraid they've bitten off more than they can chew."

Bessie realized she had to get busy and do something, or Lydia and Philippe's venture was apt to go down the drain.

Lydia and Philippe were very late coming home. Kevin and Don grumbled because supper was late, and they wanted to be taken somewhere. They were tired of sitting around the filthy house, they said.

"Clean it up," Bessie suggested. It was too bad that

88

the dinner at Malicornay hadn't worked its magic.

Dottie worked silently at the potter's wheel. She seemed to be aimlessly shaping blobs of wet clay. She apparently couldn't get the hang of it, but she was happy enough.

Thierry came by and asked Bessie if she wanted to go mushroom hunting.

They walked off to the little forest to look under the elm trees for the mushrooms called les oreilles d'orme, the ears of the elm. But they only found a few— nothing like the basketful Bessie had seen the night before Lisa left.

Thierry was not really a country boy, Bessie had learned. His family had moved from Paris not long ago, and Thierry missed city life. They were so new at La Valette that the other people in the village called his mother La Parisienne. But Thierry liked fishing and mushroom hunting and things like that. Still, he said, Paris was better.

Philippe and Lydia still hadn't come home.

Marie-Claude decided maybe they should eat, since it was dark. And it didn't get dark until ten o'clock.

They were just sitting down to supper when Lydia and Philippe arrived—with Edouard. Their car had broken down, and since they were closer to Edouard's house than to La Valette, they had called him for help. He had come to pick them up and brought them home.

"But what about your car?" Mamie asked.

Lydia and Philippe shrugged. It would be repaired, they hoped. They were to call the garage the next day. They shrugged again.

What else could go wrong? Bessie wondered.

"That means we can't go to George Sand's house tomorrow, doesn't it?" Kevin asked.

"I'm afraid it does," Lydia said. "But just as soon as the car is fixed, we'll go. . . ."

Bessie noticed that Edouard drew Marie-Claude outside and she stayed with him a long time before he finally drove away. I bet he does like Marie-Claude, thought Bessie, and I bet she likes him.

Bessie showed Philippe her negatives, but he didn't even look to see what was on them. It certainly wasn't a good time to ask for instruction in printing them.

Bessie went upstairs and tried to decide what to do. Tell Lydia and Philippe about the statues? But they were so worried now you could hardly talk to them. Tell the police? But how did you find the police in France? Unless they dropped by to check everybody's passport.

Tomorrow, though, she'd have to do something.

The next day it was raining.

Everybody sat around the breakfast table talking for what seemed to Bessie like hours. There was one small stir of excitement when the fish truck arrived and everybody went outside, either to buy fish or to see what other people bought.

Bessie couldn't find a chance to talk to Lydia alone, or anybody alone, and she didn't want to start talking about the statues in front of everybody.

Philippe said today would be a good day for everybody to work on their projects again. Who needed help? Dottie needed help at the potter's wheel, and Kevin and Don needed lots of help at the loom. Even

Mamie wanted help with her drawing of the castle's towers. "I can't get the perspective right," she said.

When everybody had scattered, Bessie stayed in the dining room with Lydia.

"Do you want to make more prints?" Lydia asked her. "Philippe will help you, I'm sure."

"That's nice," Bessie said, "but first I want to talk to you."

"What is it?"

"Well, you told me not to go into Malignon's shop. . . ."

"And you did anyway?"

"How did you know?" Bessie asked.

"Because you wouldn't have brought it up that way if you hadn't," Lydia said.

"Anyway," said Bessie, "do you remember me telling you about those statues in that little chapel near the castle?"

"Vaguely," said Lydia.

"They were very unusual," Bessie said. "They were wood and they were old, and the one of the mother and the baby had the baby smiling up at his mother and laughing. Remember?"

"Well," said Lydia, "what is it?"

"What it is is that I saw those statues when I went to Malignon's shop day before yesterday."

"Oh, there are lots of medieval wooden statues floating around the Berry," Lydia said.

"I'm sure these were the same ones," Bessie said. "Besides, Mamie and I went back to the chapel yesterday. Remember?"

"Well?" said Lydia.

"The statues are gone from the chapel," Bessie said.

"That's how I know those are the same ones in Malignon's shop."

Lydia was impressed. "So you think he stole them?" she said.

"Sure, I think he stole them," Bessie said.

"I don't think he'd do that," Lydia said. "He's a very rich man. He's an important man. He doesn't have to steal. He gets what he wants by just pushing people around."

"He takes what he wants," Bessie said. "Lots of rich people in Texas steal. I mean, just because a man is rich doesn't mean he doesn't steal."

Lydia was quiet a long time. She sat down on a bench and put her elbows on the table and leaned her head in her hands.

"Couldn't we get the police to go arrest him?" Bessie asked.

"I can't imagine that they'd believe us if we told them those statues are there," Lydia said.

"But they'd have to check it out, wouldn't they?" Bessie asked. "If we reported the statues missing from the little church?"

"I guess they would," Lydia said. "Let me talk to Philippe about it."

"When?" Bessie asked.

"As soon as I can catch him," Lydia said.

"I thought maybe you could go into Couronne and look at the statues," Bessie said.

"If *I* went there—or Philippe—they'd immediately get suspicious," Lydia said. "That wouldn't do at all."

"What about Marie-Claude?" Bessie asked.

"Well, it's raining and we don't have a car," Lydia said.

"Call Edouard," Bessie said.

"That's an idea," Lydia said. "I have to go use the phone anyway, to call the garage."

Philippe came in just then, and they talked it over, and Lydia threw a cape over her head and went out into the rain to go to Mme Poulet's.

Philippe asked Bessie if she wanted help with her prints. "Show me how to use the enlarger," Bessie said. "And you know I have a picture of those statues at Malignon's."

Philippe was very interested then, and he looked at the negative a long time. He'd help her make the print, he said. They made a test strip and then developed it, and set the timer. They used a big sheet of paper, popped it into the developer, and watched the picture emerge while the paper lay in the developer tray. Then they put it in a stop bath and then in a fix. Then they washed it.

"Do you remember the chapel by the castle?" Bessie asked Philippe.

Philippe nodded.

"Don't these look like the statues in the chapel?"

"Très semblables," Philippe said. Very like.

Edouard and François arrived in time for lunch. (There was fish from the truck.)

Kevin said something about wishing he had catsup for his fish, and this annoyed Lydia so much she almost hit him.

And Dottie said, "I do wish we would talk French all the time, the way we used to do—before *they* came," and she waved at Kevin and Don.

"Well, excuse me," said Kevin, and he got up from the table and went outside. Don followed him.

"Oh, I don't know what to do with them!" Lydia said.

"They'll get used to it," Mamie said.

"I don't think they ever will," Lydia said. "Besides, they do make it impossible to talk French."

Edouard asked what it was that Lydia wanted him to do. Lydia explained in rapid French about the statues in Malignon's shop.

Mamie and Dottie, who apparently had understood nothing, left.

"Tell Edouard where the statues are, Bessie," Lydia said.

Bessie explained exactly where they were—next to the door in the back room of Malignon's antique shop.

Lydia asked him if he'd ever seen the statues in the little chapel, and Edouard said he had and he thought he had a pretty good idea of what they looked like.

Edouard and Marie-Claude were going out the door, ready for the foray into Couronne, when Kevin came running along the front of the house, from the direction of his room, dodging the raindrops.

"Where are you going?" he asked Marie-Claude. "Can I come, too?"

Marie-Claude did not understand what he was saying and turned to Lydia, who stood in the doorway.

"No, Kevin," Lydia said. "They're going off on private business. You can't go."

She waved Marie-Claude and Edouard on. Kevin was furious.

"I think that's really very cheap of you, Lydia," he said. "It's boring here in the rain with nothing to do. I'd like to get away. I'd like to see something of France while I'm here. I want to do something."

In the middle of this tirade, just as Edouard was driving off, the little yellow police van appeared. Edouard turned and came back, and he and Marie-Claude came back into the house.

The police asked to see everyone's passport and identity papers.

They were there a long time.

They were the same two policemen who had come the first day Bessie was there, and by this time Lydia seemed to feel quite at ease with them.

She talked to them a long time, about Malignon and her carte d'identité and her carte de séjour. Bessie couldn't decide what the police thought about Lydia.

The younger policeman took the Americans' passports out to the van to radio Paris, and the other, older policeman stayed in the dining room.

Kevin, Don, Mamie, Bessie, and Dottie sat in a row on one bench and stared at him. Philippe, Marie-Claude, Lydia, Edouard, and François sat on the other side. Lydia kept on talking to him. The policeman was not hostile, but then he wasn't exactly cordial either.

When the conversation between Lydia and the policeman died down, Bessie, on an impulse, went into the darkroom and got the photograph of the statues in the shop.

"Monsieur," she said. She felt a little shy, and Bessie Hightower was not used to feeling shy.

"Mademoiselle?" he said.

She would like to show him a photograph, she said. Only she heard herself saying it in French: "Je voudrais vous montrer une photographie."

"Oui, mademoiselle," the policeman said.

"Quelqu'un a volé ces statues," she said. Someone has stolen these statues, and she went on, in French: "from the little chapel beside the château. I have seen these statues in the shop of Monsieur Malignon. In Couronne. I do not say that he stole these statues, but they are in his shop."

Now the policeman was interested. He began a question in French. And Bessie prayed with all her might—surely God understood French as well as He did English—that she would understand what he was saying.

And she did. He was merely asking her if she wanted to report the robbery. Well, she'd already reported it, hadn't she? But she merely said, "Oui, monsieur."

He took out his notebook and began to make notes. He asked her the date she had last seen the statues in the chapel, when she had first seen them, when she had seen them in the shop of M. Malignon.

"Je connais cette petite chapelle," he said. He knew the small chapel, he went on, because his grandmother had grown up in the village at the château's gates, and he had been taken to the chapel as a child.

Then he went back over the questions, asking the same ones all over again, and Bessie gave the same answers all over.

Then he asked each of the others the same questions.

Of course, no one could provide any more answers. Dottie and Kevin and Don were completely at sea— they had never even seen the chapel or Malignon's shop.

Marie-Claude, Edouard, Philippe, and Lydia had all seen the statues in the little chapel at some time or other. But nobody had paid much attention to them— except Philippe, who had guessed they were medieval and pointed them out to Lydia.

Nobody had seen the statues in the shop of M. Malignon, except Bessie.

The younger policeman came in from the van with everybody's passports in his hand. The older policeman took them and gave them out one by one, calling the names and giving them French pronunciations.

He pronounced Elizabeth Travis Hightower as though it were Ay-lee-za-bett Trah-vee Ee-to-ver, which made Bessie giggle.

Finally, he stood up to go. "Au revoir, mes amis," he said.

"Well, he called us his friends," Bessie said.

Lydia was exultant.

"Bessie, I think you've done it!" she said. "You've turned the tables. I do believe it's going to be all right."

"I don't understand anything that's going on," Kevin said crossly.

"Just relax," Lydia said. "Everything is going to be all right."

THE car wasn't ready the next day, nor was everything
else all right.

The police returned and reported coldly that they
had found no statues in the shop of M. Malignon. No
statues at all. They had searched the premises with
great care, and they had seen no statues.

"But I saw them," Bessie said. "And I have the picture to prove it." She went to get the photograph
again, and showed it to one of the policemen.

Alas, he said, the photograph did not prove that the
statues were ever in M. Malignon's shop. The statues
could have been photographed anywhere—even in this
house, he said.

"Monsieur!" said Lydia.

"Madame," said the policeman, "I only point out that
the photograph could have been made anyplace.
There is nothing in the photograph to prove that the
statues were ever in the shop."

He bowed and left.

Well, that is that, Bessie thought. So much for turning the tables on Malignon.

She went outside and walked slowly toward the lavoir, where she watched Thierry fish.

He seemed to ask nothing more of the world, she thought, than to stand around over some weedy old water trying to catch a fish. Occasionally he caught a small fish, but he always threw it back. He was after the big one.

Bessie wandered back toward Lydia's house and found Lydia outside, organizing a bicycle trip to the sabotier.

"What's a sabotier?" Bessie asked.

He was a man who made sabots, Lydia explained. Sabots were the wooden shoes that peasants used to wear and that some people still wore. He made them by hand, to order, and it was fun to visit his shop. Bessie went inside to get her camera.

Kevin and Don seemed in a very good humor, and they all started out. Thierry saw them go past the lavoir, and he ran home and got his bicycle and caught up with them.

It was a long ride to the sabotier's—farther than to Couronne. The hills made it hard work. When they got to the village where the sabotier lived, they stopped in a café and had drinks.

The sabotier welcomed them quietly and stood back while the Americans all clattered around his shop, trying on sample clogs and talking.

Bessie immediately ordered a pair of red ones, and then took pictures while Mamie and Dottie ordered plain natural ones. Kevin and Don couldn't make up their minds.

Kevin had millions of questions to ask the sabotier, and Lydia had to translate for him. He was afraid the wooden shoes might harm his feet, but then, he would like to have some. In the end, they left before he was able to make up his mind.

They would come back, Lydia said. Everyone's new clogs would be ready in a few days.

It was on the trip home that Bessie decided what to do next.

She would look for another house for Philippe and Lydia. She had a feeling they might never win their battle with Malignon. They should just move out and find another house.

Of course, there was all the work they had done on the house at La Valette. But then, they should *buy* a house! That was the thing to do. Then they wouldn't be in danger of being evicted. There was probably a way they could get the money.

It all sounded so sensible, she wondered why nobody had thought of it before.

She caught up with Thierry, who rode far in front of the group, and pedaled beside him until he noticed her. "How did your family find the house at La Valette?" she asked.

"Pure chance," Thierry said. A man who had worked with his father had told him it was going to be for sale. His father had rushed down to La Valette right away and bought it.

How could you find a house? Bessie wondered. There must be real estate agents in France. She tried to ask Thierry, but he didn't know what she was talking about. She dropped back and asked Lydia. Lydia said that a man called a notaire handled real estate sales.

"Why do you want to know?" Lydia asked.

"Just wondered," Bessie said.

Well, now, where would you find a notaire? Bessie wondered. There wasn't one in Delle. She knew every doorway in Delle by now. There must be one in Couronne.

That afternoon, she set out for Couronne. She went to her favorite sidewalk café, the one that had ice, and drank a citron pressé. She asked the waiter if there was a notaire in Couronne.

But certainly, he said, and he pointed down the street.

Bessie finished her citron pressé and made her way to the office of the notaire. She went in.

The notaire was a young man, very neatly dressed in a suit and tie. He sat behind a desk in an office with high ceilings, tall casement windows, and an armoire against the wall.

Bessie hoped her French would be up to this interview. "Je voudrais acheter une maison," she said. I want to buy a house.

"*Toi*, mademoiselle?" the notaire said. *You*, miss?

That was the trouble. Nobody would believe a thirteen-year-old girl wanted to buy a house. But why wouldn't they? Americans were crazy, weren't they?

"J'ai de l'argent," she said. I have some money. "My grandmother, who is in heaven . . ." (Well, one of her grandmothers *was* in heaven, and she had indeed left Bessie a tiny bit of money, though not enough to buy a house anywhere.) "I love France, and I would like to buy a small house, in the country. . . ."

"Tu es allemande?" the notaire said.

How could he think I'm German? Bessie wondered. "I am an American," she said proudly. "From Texas."

"Ahhh, Texas," said the notaire. "Hmmmm. Made-

102

moiselle, it is very difficult for Americans to buy property in France."

"Perhaps," she said. "But do you know of any houses for sale in the neighborhood?"

"One or two, mademoiselle," said the notaire. He hesitated, and then spoke bluntly. "I do not like to talk of business affairs with children."

"I am not a child," Bessie said. How did you say teenager in French? "Je suis une jeune fille." I am a young lady.

The notaire pointed out that a minor could not purchase a house without the consent of her parent or guardian.

But couldn't she find the house and then get her parents' consent? she asked. There would be no problem, she assured him, lying through her teeth. She would like to look at some nice houses "dans la campagne," in the country.

The notaire shook his head. But no, he said.

"But are there any houses for sale in the neighborhood?" Bessie asked. "I would like to ask that question of you."

There were a few houses for sale, the notaire said, but he would not show them to children.

Furious, Bessie left. She pedaled hard and fast, and went back down to the castle ruins. The castle ruins were beginning to seem like home.

I really like this old castle, she thought. If I were like girls in some books, I might actually sit here and dream about what had happened at the castle in the olden days, and maybe get involved in a really nice fantasy.

But Bessie Hightower had no use for fantasy. Real

life was more important, and besides, she had her work cut out for her—a hard row to hoe, as people said in Texas.

She left for La Valette.

At home, she found a cheery scene. Marie-Claude and Lydia were setting up the big table in the orchard. They were going to eat outside that night.

"That's fun," Bessie said, and she helped bring things outdoors. As they worked, she asked Lydia if she and Philippe had ever thought of buying a house.

"We have," Lydia said. "Philippe's parents say they will help us, and I've written to my parents about it. It does seem like a good idea."

"Have you been to see a notaire?" Bessie asked.

"Oh, yes," Lydia said, "but none of them have anything in our price range, or anywhere near our price range. Is that why you asked me about a notaire?"

"I guess so," Bessie said.

Houses in France were very, very hard to find, Lydia said. You had to know someone to find anything except the most expensive houses.

"How did Edouard find his house?" Bessie asked.

"He inherited it," Lydia said.

Supper started out to be fun, and Bessie took several pictures of the group at the long table under an apple tree. But Kevin and Don, as usual, ruined it. Kevin began by complaining that he hadn't had time at the sabotier's to make up his mind about his shoes. He was always being rushed, he said.

Then Don began to slap at the bugs.

"I can't stand bugs," Kevin said. "We'll have to take our supper indoors."

"There are bugs indoors, too," Bessie pointed out.

104

"Not as many," Kevin said. "But you're right. I can't see why the filthy French can't have screens on the doors." He and Don left to go indoors.

Lydia got up and left the table and started running down the lane toward Mme Poulet's house. Everyone at the table was eating silently. They saw Lydia come back and head for her house. In a minute, she came back and sat down at the table and poured herself a glass of wine.

"I've solved one of our problems," she said. "I called a taxi from Argenton. It's coming to pick up Kevin and Don and take them to the train. I gave them a refund. I can't stand them another minute."

"Were they mad?" Bessie asked.

"A little," Lydia said. "But as I said, I couldn't stand them another minute. They were spoiling it for everybody."

Surprisingly, Kevin and Don packed quickly and came outside and told everyone good-bye. They even exchanged addresses with Mamie and Bessie and Dottie.

They didn't seem bitter—in fact Bessie thought they were happy to be leaving.

When the taxi came, they jumped in and waved good-bye as they left.

"I think they were glad to leave," Mamie said in a surprised tone of voice. "That's funny. Lydia, you're great. I would never, never have had the nerve to do it, but it was the best thing in the world. You really are a good manager."

THE next day, Bessie started looking for a house herself.

She started out with her camera and a map and her
lunch in a knapsack, and rode her bicycle down the
road toward Malicornay. Might as well start somewhere, she thought.

When she saw somebody on the road, she asked if
they knew of an empty house, a house to rent or a
house for sale. They often had trouble understanding
her, and they were always astonished that an American
girl was asking questions like that. Nobody she met
knew of a house.

She would come to a small village, stop at the café if
there was one, and have a citron pressé if they had it.
If they didn't have it, she'd have a limonade. Then
she'd sip and ask if anyone knew of a house for rent or
for sale.

Each day she took another road and repeated the
same performance. A woman who ran a tiny café in
the kitchen of her home told her about a house some
distance away, and Bessie went off to look at it.

On the way, she was very excited. At last, a house. Lydia and Philippe would be so pleased.

When Bessie saw the house, she realized it was hopeless. It was an absolute, total ruin. Half the roof was gone. The windows were boarded up. The brickwork and the plaster outside needed redoing. Bessie was horrified.

But she kept on asking people about houses, although she was beginning to feel a little bit foolish.

The car was finally repaired, and Lydia and Philippe took everybody on sightseeing excursions. They went to see George Sand's house, and Bessie loved the puppet theater and she liked what she heard about George Sand, that she had worn men's clothes and smoked cigars and done what she pleased. They went to see lots of churches, some with mosaics, some with frescoes, some with famous wood carvings.

Bessie felt she was wasting time. It was fine for Mamie, for instance, to be looking at churches, but she, Bessie, ought be out doing something.

There was no further word from the police or from Malignon.

Dottie cheered up and began to turn out a few pieces of pottery that were good enough to be fired in a kiln. Philippe had meant to build his own kiln that month, he said, but he'd been too busy with the lawyers to start it. A friend of his, though, had a kiln, and Philippe promised to fire Dottie's pots.

Philippe and Bessie worked in the darkroom, and Bessie began to assemble a portfolio of prints of life in a village in the Berry. There was the woman with the geese, the sabotier, the ruined castle, all the people who lived at La Valette, and the trucks that came there. She learned how to use the agrandisseur by herself and how to develop and wash her own prints.

"I do need a better camera," she said one day.

Philippe agreed. She was ready for a camera on which she could adjust the aperture and the time.

He would lend her one of his 35-millimeter cameras, he said. Bessie accepted gratefully, and promised to be careful with it. Philippe really was the nicest person in the whole world, she decided. He and Lydia should get married and live happily ever after.

She even asked Lydia one day why they didn't get married.

"We don't believe in it," Lydia said.

"Why?" Bessie said.

"It's an outmoded institution," Lydia said. "All of us agree. Philippe. Marie-Claude."

"Edouard?"

"Oh, no. Edouard wants to get married," Lydia said.

They were still sitting around the dining table after breakfast one morning when the next blow fell.

Malignon himself appeared.

A young man beside him, he drove up in a big, shiny car and stopped in front of the house. Lydia was standing up and saw them, and her eyes widened.

"It's Malignon," she said.

Everybody jumped up to look.

"Who's that with him?" Bessie asked.

"One of his employees, I guess," Lydia said.

Malignon got out of the car and came and knocked loudly, authoritatively, on the doorpost. The door was open, but he remained outside.

"Yes?" Lydia said.

"I want to talk to you and Philippe," he said.

"Yes?" Lydia said, not asking him in.

Malignon came in anyway and brushed past her. He took charge.

"Sit down, everyone," he said. He was a sleek-looking man, fairly large for a Frenchman, dressed in an expensive silk shirt which was unbuttoned halfway down his chest.

Obediently, everyone sat down. (Why are we doing what he tells us? wondered Bessie.) Malignon began to talk. Bessie didn't understand all of it, but she got the main thrust.

They were going to have to move. Malignon was giving them until the end of July—then they had to be out.

"We have guests coming in August," Lydia said. "From America. This is our business, our livelihood. We can't move."

That did not matter, Malignon said. They would have to move.

"But we have a lease," Lydia said.

"The lease no longer operates," Malignon said coldly. "You have received notice before, and I have come to assure you personally that this is a serious matter. I speak for the owner. You must be out of here by the first of August."

Lydia always tried to be reasonable with everyone, and she began to explain, as though for the first time, that they *couldn't* move out, that they had too much at stake in the house, that they had guests coming, that they had a lease.

"I say to you that none of these things is important,"

109

Malignon said. "You must leave. If you do not leave, you will be thrown out and your possessions placed in the road."

A gasp went around the table.

Malignon nodded slowly. He wished to be amiable, he said. But they must leave. He stood up, held out his hand. Automatically, Lydia shook it. Malignon went around the table, shaking hands with each person in turn. Until he came to Bessie. Bessie folded her arms and shook her head at him. She wasn't about to shake his hand, she thought. He was a bully and a thief.

Malignon left.

The visit had lasted five minutes, but the effect was devastating. Mamie and Dottie began to talk of going home at once. Philippe went outside and lay down in the grass under an apple tree. Lydia stood around for a minute and then went to Mme Poulet's to call the lawyer.

She came back, looking whipped.

"What are you going to do?" Bessie asked.

"I don't know," Lydia said. "I don't know. The lawyer says perhaps we should move. . . ."

Bessie decided she'd better find them a house—and in a hurry.

She started out on her bicycle and took a road that she thought she hadn't taken before. She realized, though, that it was the road to the village where Jules, the sorcerer, lived, and she decided to stop by his house.

Why not consult him? she asked herself. They needed a little sorcery.

She got off her bicycle and knocked on Jules' doorpost. He was sitting at the table, sipping wine. His dog lay at his feet.

"Bonjour, mademoiselle," he said.

"Bonjour, monsieur."

She didn't know what to say next. Jules got up and poured some water in a glass, added a drop of wine, and handed it to her.

"Merci," she said. She sat down at the table with him.

I would like to ask your advice, she began slowly in French. It was easier than she had thought. She talked to him about Philippe and Lydia and Malignon. He knew the situation—but he didn't know of Malignon's visit. Bessie told him that she had been looking for a house for Philippe and Lydia. It seemed they might be able to buy their own house. But now it was absolutely necessary that they find something in a hurry.

Jules was quiet a long time, and Bessie wondered if he was interested—or if he'd gone to sleep or passed out from the wine.

But Jules hadn't passed out. In a few minutes, he spoke. There was a house for sale, he said. He stopped. It had been empty a long time, he added finally. He spoke slowly for her benefit. And when Bessie didn't understand him, he repeated what he'd said even more slowly.

The house was in a village called Luis, he said. He told her how to get there. The house was old. It would need some repairs. But it was for sale. And it was empty now.

Bessie thanked him. She took his picture, glad that she had the 35-millimeter camera so she could take it indoors without a flash.

She set out to find Luis. It was so small it wasn't on the Michelin map, but she thought she had seen a sign marked "Luis" somewhere. She followed Jules' directions and found Luis—and the empty house.

111

She couldn't believe it when she saw it. It was the same dilapidated wreck that the woman with the café in her kitchen had told her about some time before. Well, too bad, she thought. Jules was a washout as a sorcerer, she thought.

She went home and found everybody gone, except Lydia, and she was just leaving.

"Hurry, Bessie!" she said. "We have to help Monsieur Brodeau with the hay!"

"What?"

Lydia stopped to explain hastily that in the country everybody helped everybody else get in his hay, especially at times like this when it looked as though it might rain. Bessie hurried with Lydia to the hay field, where the others were already at work.

M. Brodeau drove the tractor down the field, where the hay was already baled. Their job was to throw the bales up on the trailer behind the tractor. It wasn't bad work at all, Bessie thought.

When they had filled the trailer, they all got on top of the hay and rode back to the village and helped put it in the loft of M. Brodeau's barn. Then they rode back to the field to get more bales.

They finished just before it started to rain, and they all went back to the Brodeau house, where wine (and soda for Bessie) flowed. Everyone forgot about Malignon and evictions and impôts and cartes de séjour.

Bessie, though, kept her mind on the problem. She would have to go further afield to look for houses, she decided. She'd go to Couronne tomorrow.

THE next morning, Bessie told Lydia about her visit to Jules.

"He told me about this old house and I became very excited," Bessie said in French. "I knew it was the house for you—until I saw it. It's falling down."

"Where is it?" Lydia asked.

Bessie told her, and then said she thought she'd go into Couronne today. "Maybe I can find a house on the other side of Couronne," she said.

"Bessie, you are magnificent," Lydia said. "You're as worried about our problems as we are."

"I might want to come back sometime," Bessie said, "and I want you to have a house for me to come to."

She packed her knapsack as always—camera, lunch, map.

As she pedaled out toward the paved road, Thierry came up beside her on his bicycle and asked where she was going.

"A Couronne," she said.

Thierry shrugged, circled around her, and went back to the village.

Bessie pedaled on alone. At Couronne, she stopped

for her usual citron pressé. She asked the waiter if he knew of a house for sale. He didn't.

Bessie headed out of Couronne and couldn't resist the road to the castle. She'd just make a short visit, she decided, and take some pictures with the 35-millimeter camera.

When she got there, she sat down and ate her lunch. It was still early, and she'd be hungry later, but she ate her bread and cheese and sat on the clover and looked about her. Then she got out the camera and took pictures of the stairway, which she had only been able to photograph with a flash before. Then she took pictures of the pointed windows, the gate, the parapets on the outer wall . . . everything.

She went in the ruins of the donjon and looked up at the walls with the niches in them. Poking around some stones by the chimney, she noticed for the first time a small door and a stairway that went down. Following it, she found herself in a small, dry room.

And then she found it—treasure!

Real treasure, she thought to herself when she stumbled over the vases and paintings and candlesticks piled neatly in one corner and covered with a tarpaulin.

Then she saw the wooden statues—one of them the mother with the baby laughing up at her. She was sure they were the statues from the little chapel, the statues she had seen in Malignon's antique shop.

Malignon was here, Bessie thought.

She went outside to think it over. Already, she wished she hadn't eaten her lunch. She needed brain food now.

It seemed obvious: The things were stolen. Malignon must be a mighty thief. And because she'd spotted the statues in the antique shop, he was hiding the stuff here for some reason.

She went back to the room under the donjon. It was too dark to take a picture without a flash, even with Philippe's good camera and the lens wide open. And she didn't have a flash attachment. Maybe she could take a time exposure, she thought—but she had never really understood about time exposures.

Then she had an idea. She took the wooden statues upstairs to the donjon, which had plenty of light, and photographed them with the pointed windows and the ruined wall as a background. There, she thought, the police couldn't say the photograph could have been taken anywhere. She was taking the statues back down when she heard a car.

Bessie froze. She realized she had never seen anybody else at the castle. It was off the tourist track. It must be Malignon. She shoved the statues under the tarpaulin, grabbed her knapsack, and sped back up to ground level. She pushed through the bushes to the tower with the broken stairway.

She waited there, and heard men talking outside the castle walls. She climbed up the broken treads of the stairway, peered out the narrow slit window, and saw two men with a truck labeled *Poterie Malignon*.

It was as plain as day, Bessie thought.

The men came into the castle, and in a few minutes they went out, each carrying some of the treasure. Bessie picked up the camera and aimed it through the narrow window, just as a marksman in the Middle Ages would have aimed his arrow. She got a good picture of the men putting the things in the truck.

It took several trips for the men to load everything on the truck, and Bessie got several pictures.

When the men were through, they closed the doors to the truck, and one of them pointed to Bessie's bicycle, lying beside the gate to the castle.

Good grief, thought Bessie. Will they search the castle and find me?

Apparently not. One of the men opened the truck again, and the other picked up the bicycle and shoved it inside.

They drove away, taking Bessie's bicycle with them.

Well, that was pretty rotten, Bessie thought. It was bad enough to steal statues from a church, but to take a kid's bicycle was as low as you could get.

Bessie climbed down the stairs and walked back out to the courtyard. She sat down on the clover and thought about what to do next.

Eventually, she supposed, someone would come looking for her. She had told Lydia she was going to Couronne, and she had told Thierry, too.

But Bessie Hightower was not one who was content to sit and wait to be rescued. She got up, shouldered her knapsack, and prepared to walk back to La Valette.

Then she stopped and stepped into the shadow of the ruined donjon. There she unloaded her camera and put the used film in her jeans pocket. She reloaded the camera and put it in her knapsack. She wanted to keep the film as safe as possible.

BESSIE stopped in Couronne and bought some sausage at the charcuterie and some more bread at the boulangerie. She ate them at the café while she drank another citron pressé.

She thought about Malignon and wondered where his men were taking the statues and the other things. Surely he wasn't taking them back to the shop. Even though it was unlikely, Bessie decided to check. Shouldering her knapsack, she walked down the narrow streets until she came to the antique shop. Walking past it, she saw the blonde lady standing by the door, staring out at the street.

"Bonjour, madame," Bessie said, and walked on by.

"Mademoiselle," said the lady.

Bessie turned at the corner and went up the alley to get to the back of the shop. There were no trucks or vans at all parked there, and the back doors of the gift shop and the antique shop were firmly shut. The window of the antique shop was closed and shuttered, she noticed.

Well, I didn't think I'd find them here, Bessie thought, and she began the walk back to La Valette.

Six miles, Bessie found out, was a long way to walk. As she plodded along, she wondered whether she should have tried to talk to the police in Couronne. But I don't know where you find the police, she thought. They just appear. I've never seen them in Couronne. And the city hall looks like a château and I've never seen police around it . . . just some old clerks coming and going.

When she got home, Philippe and Lydia weren't there.

"They went to see Philippe's parents," Mamie said. "They wanted to talk to them."

"When will they be home?" Bessie asked.

"Tomorrow," Mamie said.

"Good grief," Bessie said.

"What's the matter?" Mamie said.

"I'm glad I didn't wait in Couronne for them to come and get me," Bessie said. "Somebody stole my bicycle."

"My goodness," said Mamie.

"And I wanted Philippe to help me with some film," Bessie said.

"Now you don't need help in the darkroom, do you?" Mamie said. "Everybody says you're doing remarkably well."

"I guess so," Bessie said. "Where's Marie-Claude?"

"Out with Edouard," Mamie said.

"Oh, that's good," Bessie said. "I mean, I wish she were here . . . but I think she and Edouard ought to get together."

Mamie said nothing to this.

Bessie went in the darkroom. If Marie-Claude had been there, she would have asked her about calling the police. But she did not want to tell Mamie what had happened. Mamie and Dottie were skittish. They might get scared and they might leave. Bessie didn't want Lydia to lose any more paying guests.

Bessie got out the tank and the reel. I'd better do it right this time, she thought. She turned out the light, locked the door, and took the film from her pocket. The 35-millimeter film was a lot easier to thread on the reel than the Instamatic film, that was for sure.

Once the film was in the tank, she turned on the light and started mixing the developer. She had a hard time getting the temperature right. She had to heat some water in the kitchen and bring it into the dark-room and set the beaker of developer in a pan of hot water until it was warm enough.

Finally, the negatives were washed, and she took them outside and looked at them in the sunlight. The pictures of the men loading the objects into the van looked perfect to her.

Hot dog, we've got him now! Bessie thought.

But, of course, they didn't have him yet.

Bessie hung the negatives up to dry and went back into the dining room. A car drove up outside. It was Edouard—but he didn't get out. Marie-Claude got out of the car, slammed the door, and stalked toward the house. Edouard drove away.

"What's the matter?" Bessie asked.

"C'est normal," Marie-Claude said.

Bessie told her about the van and the statues at the castle and the bicycle.

"La poterie!" said Marie-Claude. She was sure they'd taken the things to the pottery.

119

Malignon's pottery was on the other side of Couronne. There was a big warehouse and shipping room there, too. It must be where they had the things now. They could pack them for shipping overseas and get them out of the country with no one the wiser.

Marie-Claude thought it was time to call the police. She went over to Mme Poulet's to use the telephone.

Bessie went back to the darkroom to make the prints. She made contact prints and test strips, clocked the exposure time carefully, and timed the prints in developer, the stop bath, and fixer.

Some of the prints were marvelous. The one where the men were loading the statues in the van was especially good. So was the one of the statues in the donjon with the ruined wall in the background.

The police came very quickly—the same two policemen, one young, one old.

By this time, Bessie had told Mamie and Dottie what had happened, and all four of them sat at the dining table with the policemen.

The police looked at Bessie's photographs carefully.

"You did these alone, mademoiselle?" asked the older one.

"Oui, monsieur, I have learned it since I have come to France," Bessie said.

The police were impressed. They asked if they could take them along.

Bessie said, but of course.

Then the policemen asked Bessie questions. If she didn't understand their French, they repeated it. She answered as well as she could. Sometimes Marie-Claude could help her. Once Mamie even furnished a word.

Bessie thought she told everything—several times. The hidden objects in the castle . . . the van coming . . . the men loading the van . . . and the last-minute theft of her bicycle. She described the bicycle in minute detail—she knew it as well as she knew her horse.

"And you, mademoiselle, you have walked from the ruined castle to La Valette?"

"Oui, monsieur," she said.

"I didn't know that," Mamie said.

Then the policemen asked the others if they knew anything. They didn't. They had a long conversation with Marie-Claude in rapid French which Bessie couldn't understand. They asked about Philippe and Lydia. Then they asked to see the Americans' passports and Marie-Claude's carte d'identité. The younger policeman took the three passports outside to the yellow van once more.

While he was gone, the older one had a glass of wine and chatted with Marie-Claude and, sometimes, the others.

After a long time, the young one came back with the passports.

"Clean again," said Bessie.

The policemen left.

"Do you think they believed me?" Bessie asked Marie-Claude.

"Je ne sais pas," Marie-Claude said, shrugging hugely. "Allons," she said. It was time for dinner. And she would show them, three American ladies, how to make a country omelette, with potatoes.

Philippe and Lydia came home the next day while Bessie was in the darkroom, making more prints of the statues and the castle. She heard them laughing and talking in the dining room. Marie-Claude exclaimed in French, and it sounded as though something exciting had happened.

As soon as she could safely open the door, Bessie went out to see what was going on.

"Bessie!" Lydia said. "You did it!"

"Did they catch him?" Bessie asked.

"Catch who?" Lydia said. "You solved our problems, Bess!"

"How?" Bessie asked.

"We've bought the house," Lydia said.

"Bought the house?" Bessie couldn't understand. "What house?"

"The house in Luis you told us about," Lydia said. "It was the bargain of centuries—just twenty-five thousand francs."

"But it doesn't have a roof," Bessie said. "It's falling down."

"But Philippe can fix it," Lydia said. "You don't un-

122

derstand. Philippe can build anything. We're so thrilled we can't stand it. We went by to see it on an impulse when we were on our way to Philippe's family's house. We loved the village and we loved the house. It has all these little barns and outbuildings we can use for studios. The lady next door told us who owned it and how to reach her. We drove over to see the owner, and when we found out how much it was we couldn't believe it. We went on to see Philippe's family, and they're lending us enough to buy it. I called my parents, and they'll lend us enough to fix it up. Just think—we'll have our own little house. We needn't worry about being evicted. We can have our looms and darkroom and everything. Philippe can build his kiln. We won't have to move ever again."

"But you needn't bother now," Dottie said.

"What do you mean?" Lydia asked.

"We caught Malignon," Dottie said.

"Bess-ee l'a attrapé," Marie-Claude said. Bessie caught him. She told Philippe and Lydia what had happened at the castle.

"That's incredible!" said Lydia. "Bess-ee tu es magnifique." She hugged Bessie.

"Oh, we still need to buy a house," Lydia said. "It's foolish for us to do the things we do to a rented house. Besides, the French law is so slow, it will take years to prosecute Malignon—if they prosecute him."

Everyone agreed that it was a very good thing to buy a house.

"We should celebrate," Mamie said.

"We must," Lydia said. "We'll have a fête tonight."

"But what about the impôt and the carte de séjour?" Bessie asked.

"Philippe's father has found us another lawyer who

thinks he can handle the income tax thing. It's just a matter of clearing up a misunderstanding," Lydia said. "And as for the carte de séjour—well, we've thought of a neat way to solve that one."

Lydia took Philippe's hand and looked at him adoringly. "Let's tell them," she said. "Disons-le leur."

"Certainement," Philippe said.

"Philippe and I are going to get married," she said. "That way I can stay in France as long as I like. I don't ever have to leave."

"Hooray!" said Bessie.

Everyone else cheered, except Marie-Claude, who looked disgusted. "Le mariage—ffft," she said.

"Marie-Claude doesn't believe in marriage," Lydia said.

"Edouard does," Philippe said.

"Edouard—ffft," said Marie-Claude.

"Une fête. Une fête." Lydia chanted and danced around the room like a madwoman. "We'll invite Edouard and François and Madame Poulet and Jacques and Joseph and Madame Brodeau and Monsieur Brodeau and Thierry and La Parisienne. . . ."

"And Jules," Bessie said.

"And Jules, the sorcerer," Lydia said. "Tout le monde, the whole world will come to our fête."

"Bess-ee!" It was Mme Poulet at the door. Bessie had a telephone call—from America.

"Good grief," Bessie said. She ran down the lane ahead of Mme Poulet and went in Mme Poulet's kitchen.

She picked up the phone and answered it. "Hello."

There was a babble of French. An operator was trying to make sure this was Bess-ee Eye-Tover.

Then Bessie heard her father's voice on the phone.

"What's the matter?" he said. "Are you all right?"

"Of course I'm all right," Bessie said.

"We haven't had but one letter from you," Mr. Hightower said. "And we thought we'd better see if you were all right. Your mother has been about to have a stroke."

"I'm fine," Bessie said. "I'm having a wonderful time. I just haven't had time to write."

Bessie's mother came on the phone and wanted to know if she was all right. Bessie told her yes, she was all right. She was fine. She was having a wonderful time.

"What have you been doing?" Mrs. Hightower asked.

"I've learned a lot of French," Bessie said. "And I've—" She hesitated. All she had done ran through her mind . . . found a house, caught a thief, gotten lost, met a sorcerer . . . but none of it could be explained over the transatlantic telephone to her *parents.* "I've learned photography!" she said. "I know how to develop film and make prints. And I need a better camera."

Bessie could hear her mother talking to her father, and her father came on the line again.

"I'm glad you've learned photography, Bessie," he said. "I can't wait to tell old Clark Haynes you can do it. He thinks he's the only one west of the Sabine that can turn the lights off in a darkroom. And you want a better camera?"

"Yes, sir," Bessie said.

Her mother came back on the line to ask again if she was well. "I'm fine, Mama," she said. "Can I stay another month?"

"Oh, no, Bessie, we miss you too much," her mother said. Again she spoke to Bessie's father.

"No sir-ree, bobtail," Mr. Hightower said. "You cannot stay another month. You come on home when you're supposed to. If you don't, I'm coming—we're all coming—over there to get you."

"D'accord," Bessie said.

The operator came on the phone as Bessie heard her parents saying "What?" "What?" The operator said something unintelligible and cut them off.

Bessie grinned and hung up the phone.

Was everything all right? Mme Poulet asked Bessie in French.

"Oui, madame, merci," Bessie said, skipping down the lane toward home.

She heard Thierry shouting behind her. She couldn't understand what he was saying. She turned around and saw him coming from the lavoir, holding high the big, big fish.

"Juh lay uh!" He shouted it over and over. "Juh lay uh! Juh lay uh!"

He ran past her and past Lydia's house, still shouting "Juh lay uh!" and ran into his own house.

Everyone in the village came out to see him go by— Jacques, Joseph, Mme Brodeau and M. Brodeau and Gabrielle and Mme Poulet and Lydia and Philippe and Marie-Claude and Edouard and Mamie and Dottie.

"What's he saying?" Bessie asked Lydia. "I can't understand it."

Lydia went inside and wrote it down for the other Americans: *Je l'ai eu,* which means "I have it" or "I got it."

"That's something else to celebrate at the fête," Bessie said.

The fête was a great success. Everyone came—except Jules, the sorcerer. He never left home, he told Lydia.

126

Philippe set up tables in the orchard and hung candles in bottles from the trees.

Edouard, made resolute and fervent by the news that Philippe and Lydia were going to be married, persuaded Marie-Claude to marry him—or come live with him—Bessie couldn't be sure which. But they both looked happy.

She sat down at a table, drinking her citron pressé with ice—"This is really Bess-ee's fête," Lydia had said, "and we have to have ice"—and Bessie felt as happy as Edouard looked.

Then the police came.

"Oh, good grief," said Bessie, "I hope they didn't come to check our passports."

They didn't.

They joined the fête, and the older one sat down with Lydia and Bessie and had a long talk with them. He held Bessie's hand and called her "ma fille" and patted her on the head from time to time.

It was an unofficial visit, he said. He went on to tell them that the police had shown Malignon the photograph of the men loading the statues on the truck.

Malignon had said that was a perfectly normal operation for an antique dealer. He said the objects were not stolen. The police had then asked him why the objects were at the ruined castle.

Malignon had said he knew nothing of that, that they should ask the men who had been using his truck, and he gave the police their names and addresses.

The police went to see those men, and when the men realized that Malignon was going to let them take the blame for handling stolen goods—and all the goods were stolen—they told the police everything about Malignon's businesses. His secret business was buying and picking up stolen antiques and shipping them to America. The antique shop existed almost entirely as a front for stolen art and bric-a-brac. The pottery was a real business, but it provided excellent cover for shipping various illicit things to America.

Bessie asked the police why Malignon had hidden the things in the castle.

It was not Malignon but his employees who had panicked, the police said. The men were alarmed when the blonde woman told them about Bessie photographing things in the back room. They had moved all the stolen things to the pottery. Then, when the police came to ask about the statues, they had moved everything from the pottery to the castle, where they thought it would be safe from discovery for a short period until it could be shipped off.

Would Malignon go to jail? Bessie asked.

It was too early to say, the policemen said. The older one assured Lydia that Malignon would be too busy during the next month to worry about the house at La Valette. "You will be able to finish the season here, I'm sure," he told her.

But, he added, it was a good thing they had bought their own house for next year.

"But what about the bicycle?" Bessie asked.

The bicycle was confiscated at the pottery, along with all the other things. The antiques had been packed up and were ready to go overseas in cartons of dishes from the pottery. Eventually, Lydia would get her bicycle back and the statues would go back to the little church—but it would all take time.

Thierry returned just then, in a fury.

The cat, he said, had eaten his big fish.

"Quel dommage," Bessie said.

Everyone tried to cheer Thierry up—but it was hard work.

Bessie sipped her citron pressé and decided she really had to stay another month.

And if her family came to get her, that might be fun, too. She'd be glad to see them. She could take Sam and Dan to the sabotier's, and they could all have red sabots. She could show them the ruined castle and the puppet theater at George Sand's house. She could take her mother to the antique shop. And her father—well, she would take her father to meet Jules, the sorcerer . . . and see what those two made of each other. . . .